"Tanya, are you okay?" he asked again.

Her breath shuddered out in a ragged sigh. She must have been holding it, and she murmured, "I think so..."

But he heard the doubt in her voice and eased up so she could roll over and face him. "Were you hit?" he asked. He ran his hands down her sides, checking for wounds. Just for wounds...

But he found soft curves and lean muscles instead. Heat tingled in his hands and in other parts of his body. A few minutes ago he'd thought she was going to kiss him. Their mouths had been only a breath apart, but maybe that was because he'd leaned down—because he'd wanted to kiss her so badly his gut had twisted.

The woman got to him as no one else ever had. And that made her dangerous—almost as dangerous as the shooter.

GROOM UNDER FIRE

—

LISA CHILDS

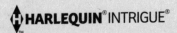

HARLEQUIN® INTRIGUE®

Recycling programs for this product may not exist in your area.

To my wonderful groom—Philip Tyson— thanks for an amazing first year of marriage. And to the woman who raised him to be the wonderful man he is, Shirley Tyson—thank you for being such a loving and supportive mother. You are a phenomenal woman, and I am so lucky to have you as a mother-in-law.

ISBN-13: 978-0-373-69767-0

GROOM UNDER FIRE

Copyright © 2014 by Lisa Childs

Printed in U.S.A.

www.Harlequin.com

ABOUT THE AUTHOR

Bestselling, award-winning author Lisa Childs writes paranormal and contemporary romance for Harlequin. She lives on thirty acres in Michigan with her two daughters, a talkative Siamese and a long-haired Chihuahua who thinks she's a rottweiler. Lisa loves hearing from readers, who can contact her through her website, www.lisachilds.com, or snail-mail address, P.O. Box 139, Marne, MI 49435.

Books by Lisa Childs

CAST OF CHARACTERS

Cooper Payne—When the former military man joins his family's personal protection business, his first assignment—protecting a bride—might become his last.

Tanya Chesterfield—She has known and loved Cooper Payne since they were kids, but all he'd ever wanted was to be her friend—until he's forced to protect her from the maniac threatening her.

Stephen Wochholz—Tanya's fiancé disappears the day before their wedding. Has he been kidnapped, or has he decided he wants more than half of the Chesterfield inheritance?

Rochelle Chesterfield—Tanya's sister resents her—enough to try to get rid of her and keep all the Chesterfield inheritance to herself?

Benedict Bradford—Tanya and Rochelle's grandfather has found a way to manipulate them from beyond the grave.

Arthur Gregory—Benedict Bradford's lawyer may be carrying out his client's wishes but he has an agenda of his own.

Logan Payne—The oldest Payne sibling runs the security business, but he has secrets that might be putting himself and his family in danger.

Parker Payne—The family playboy wants to help his brother protect the bride, but he winds up at risk himself.

Nikki Payne—The baby and only female of the Payne siblings, Nikki is determined to prove she's just as tough as her brothers.

Penny Payne—The Payne family matriarch is not part of her children's security business. As a wedding planner, she believes in another kind of security—happily ever after—and she's not above taking advantage of a situation to ensure her kids have happy marriages.

Prologue

Their petals dried and brittle and as black as tar, the roses arrived the day after the announcement was printed in the paper. There were a dozen of them in the box, the thorny stems twisted around each other like barbed wire.

Tanya Chesterfield's finger bled from the one she had been foolish enough to touch. Crimson droplets fell onto the white envelope of the card that had come with the *gift*.

Her hand trembled as she fumbled to open the envelope. Maybe she should have just tossed it and the flowers into the trash. But she had to see if it was as threatening as the other notes she'd received anytime she had seriously dated anyone the past ten years.

She wasn't just dating now, though. She was engaged. And it was that engagement announcement that she pulled from the envelope.

The picture of her and her intended groom had been desecrated with a big black *X*. But that wasn't all the marker had scratched out on the announcement. The date of the wedding had been changed to date of: *DEATH*.

Chapter One

"You're messing with me," Cooper Payne accused his older brother. He hadn't been gone so long that he'd forgotten how they all handled any emotional and uncomfortable situation—with humor and teasing.

"I'm giving you an assignment," Logan said, but he was focused on the papers on his desk as if unwilling to meet Cooper's stare. "Isn't that what you wanted?"

After his honorable discharge from the Marines, he had come home to River City, Michigan, in order to join the family business. The business his brother had started: private security protection. Not his mother's business: weddings.

"I want a *real* assignment," Cooper clarified as he paced the small confines of Logan's dark-paneled office. "Not some trick our mother put you up to."

"Trick?" Logan asked, his usually deep voice rising with fake innocence. "Why would you think it's a trick?"

Frustration clutched at his stomach, knotting his guts. "Because Mom's been trying to get me to go to this damn wedding before I even got on a plane to head back…"

"Home," Logan finished for him. "You're home. And Tanya Chesterfield and Stephen Wochholz are your friends. Why wouldn't you want to attend their wedding?"

Because the thought of Tanya marrying *any* man—let

alone Stephen—made him physically sick. He shook his head. "We were friends in high school," Cooper reminded his brother and himself. "That was a dozen years ago."

And as beautiful as Tanya was, it was a miracle that she wasn't already married with a couple of kids. It wasn't as if she would have been pining over him. They hadn't shared more than a couple of kisses in high school before agreeing that they were better as friends just as she and Stephen were. But now she was marrying Stephen...

They made sense, though. More sense than he and Tanya ever would have. She was a damned heiress to billions and he was an ex-marine working for his big brother.

Maybe...

Logan was focused on him now, studying him through narrowed blue eyes. Cooper looked so much like Logan and his twin, with the same blue eyes and black hair, that people had often questioned if they were actually triplets. But Cooper was eighteen months younger than Parker and Logan. And they never let him forget it.

Finally Logan spoke, "Stephen still considers you a friend. He requested you be his best man."

"How do you know that?" he asked. Before his brother could reply, he answered his own question, "Mom..." As much as he loved her, the woman was infuriating. "She's obsessed with this damn wedding!"

"Weddings are her business," Logan replied with pride.

For years their mother had put all her energy and love into her family—taking on the roles of both mother and father after her police-officer husband had been killed in the line of duty fifteen years ago. But when her youngest—and only girl—had gone off to college, she had found a new vocation—saving the church where she and Cooper's father had been married from demolition and turning it into a wedding venue with her as planner.

"And *security* is our business," Cooper said. His brother had promised him a job with Payne Protection the minute his enlistment ended. He had even brought him directly to the office from the airport, but that had been a couple of days ago and he had yet to give him a job. Until tonight...

"That's why you need to get over to the church," Logan told him.

"For security? At a wedding?" He snorted his derision.

"Tanya is the granddaughter of a billionaire," Logan needlessly reminded him.

As if Cooper hadn't been brutally aware of the differences between her lifestyle and his, her grandfather had pointed out that a fatherless kid like him with no prospects for the future had nothing to offer an heiress like Tanya. Benedict Bradford had wanted a doctor or lawyer for his eldest granddaughter—a man worthy of her. He hadn't considered a soldier who might not make it through his deployments worthy of Tanya. Neither had Cooper. The old man had been dead for years now, but Benedict Bradford would have approved of Stephen, who had become a corporate attorney.

"Being a billionaire's granddaughter never put her in danger before," Cooper said. Or his mother definitely would have told him about it. And if that had been the case, he wouldn't have waited until his enlistment ended before coming home.

Logan lifted up his cell phone and turned it toward Cooper. "This might say otherwise..."

Coop peered at a dark, indiscernible image on the small screen. "What the hell is that?"

"Black roses," Logan replied with a shudder of revulsion. "They were delivered to the church today."

"That doesn't say danger," Cooper insisted. "That says mix-up at the florist's."

Logan shook his head. "The wedding's tomorrow, so the real flowers aren't being delivered until morning."

Cooper arched an eyebrow now, questioning how his brother was so knowledgeable of wedding policy and procedure.

"It's *Mom,*" Logan said. "Of course we help her out from time to time. Like now. You need to get to the church."

"You just said the wedding's tomorrow."

"So that means the rehearsal's tonight," Logan said with a snort of disgust at Cooper's ignorance.

But he'd already been gone—first to boot camp and then a base in Okinawa—when their mother had bought the old church. He had no knowledge of weddings and absolutely no desire to learn about them.

"So if someone wants to stop the wedding from happening," Logan continued, "they'll make their move tonight."

Someone wanted to stop the wedding. But Cooper had no intention of making a move. Nothing had changed since high school. There had been nothing between Tanya and him then but friendship. And there was less than nothing between them now. He hadn't talked to her in years.

But if she was in danger…

HER HAND SHOOK as Tanya lifted the zippered garment bag containing her wedding gown toward the hook hanging on the wall of the bride's dressing room. It wasn't the weight of the yards of satin and lace that strained her muscles but the weight of the guilt bearing down on her shoulders. *I can't do this! It's not right...*

But neither was her grandfather's manipulation. Even a decade after his death, the old man hadn't given up trying to control his family. A couple of decades ago, he had bought off Tanya's father, so that he had left her mother and her and her sister, forcing them to move in with her grandfather.

That place had been the exact opposite of the bright room in which Tanya stood now. The bride's dressing room was all white wainscoting and soft pink paint. That house had been cold and dark. She shuddered at just the thought of the mausoleum. But then she smiled as she remembered who had called the drafty mansion that first. Cooper Payne.

He had kissed her there—after he'd pushed her up against one of the pillars of the front porch. That kiss had happened more than a dozen years ago, but her heart beat erratically at the memory. It had never pounded that hard over any other kiss. Her very first kiss...

Maybe that was why it had meant so much. Maybe that was why, even though it had been years since she'd seen him, she thought so often of Cooper Payne. It was probably good that he'd turned down Stephen's request to be his best man. Good that he wasn't going to be standing there when she followed through with this charade.

She wouldn't be able to utter her vows—to *lie*—with him looking at her. Not that he'd ever been able to tell when she was lying...

He had believed her when she'd agreed with him that the kiss—and the few that had followed it—had been a mistake, that they were only meant to be friends. She had nodded and smiled even while her teenage heart had been breaking.

Maybe it was the memory of that pain that had kept her from ever falling in love again. But then there had also been those threats. Stephen was convinced they were empty. But what if they weren't?

Should she risk it, as Stephen had advised? Or should she forfeit her inheritance?

She glanced into the antique mirror that stood next to where the garment bag hung, but she quickly turned away from the image of blond hair and haunted green eyes. She couldn't even look at herself right now. If she followed through with this farce, she would never be able to look at herself again.

She breathed a ragged sigh. She wouldn't miss the money; it had never been hers anyway. But she'd had plans for it—good plans, charitable plans…

Her grandfather had never practiced any charity—not even at home. Benedict Bradford had really been a mean old miser. So giving away his money would have been the perfect revenge for how he'd treated her mother and her and her sister.

But a wedding shouldn't be about revenge. Or money. Or even charity. It should be about love. And while Tanya loved her groom, she wasn't *in* love with him.

"I—I can't do this…"

Not the wedding. Not even the damn rehearsal. She crossed the room and jerked open the door to the vestibule and nearly ran into Cooper Payne's mother. Petite and slender with coppery-red hair and warm brown eyes, Mrs. Payne was exactly the opposite of her tall, dark, muscular sons. Only the youngest—her daughter—looked like her.

"What's the matter, honey?" the older woman asked as she gripped Tanya's trembling arms. "Are you all right?"

Tanya shook her head. "No, nothing's right…"

"I know the rest of the wedding party hasn't shown up yet, but there's no rush," Mrs. Payne assured her, her voice as full of warmth and comfort as her eyes. "Reverend James and I—"

She didn't care about the rest of the wedding party. "Stephen—is Stephen here?"

Mrs. Payne nodded. "I showed him to the groom's quarters a while ago, so that he could stow his tux there for tomorrow, like you've stowed your dress. Then you'll have less to worry about for the ceremony."

There was not going to be a ceremony. But Tanya couldn't tell anyone that until she'd told Stephen. He'd concocted this crazy scheme in the first place because he was her friend, because he'd always been there for her. But she couldn't take advantage of that friendship, of him.

"Where are the groom's quarters?" she asked.

"You need to wait until the others show," Mrs. Payne said. "So that the rehearsal can proceed just as the ceremony will tomorrow."

"No, I—I need to talk to Stephen," she insisted. "Now." Before the farce went any further.

Mrs. Payne's brown eyes widened. But after having worked with so many happy couples over the years, she must have realized something was off with them—that Tanya was hardly an ecstatic bride. "The groom's quarters are behind the altar."

Tanya crossed the vestibule and opened the heavy oak doors to the church. Since night had already fallen, the stained-glass windows were dark. The only light came from the sconces on the walls, casting shadows from the pews into the aisle. So she didn't notice that the red velvet runner was tangled. She tripped over it, catching herself before she dropped to her knees. That was weird—usually Mrs. Payne never missed a thing. No detail escaped her attention.

The wedding planner had worked so hard that guilt tugged at Tanya. She hated to disappoint the woman. But she couldn't go through with a lie.

Stephen would understand that. It wasn't as if he thought of her as anything other than a friend either, so he wouldn't be hurt.

The door to the room behind the altar stood ajar. She pushed it open to darkness. "Stephen?"

Had he changed his mind, too? She didn't blame him, but she doubted that he would have just left without talking to her first. She fumbled along the wall, feeling for the switch, when her fingers smeared across something wet. That wasn't something Mrs. Payne would have missed either. The chapel was spotless.

Tanya flipped on the switch, bathing the room in light—and discovered it had already been bathed in blood. It was spattered across the floor, the couch and the wall. Panic and fear rose up at the horror, choking her, so that she could barely utter the scream burning her throat.

COOPER HEARD IT. Even though the scream wasn't loud, the sheer terror of it pierced his heart. He ran past his mother, who was already halfway down the aisle of the church—and toward the danger. Years had passed since he'd heard it, but he had instinctively recognized Tanya's voice.

"Stay here," he ordered his mother as he reached beneath his leather jacket and pulled his weapon from the arm holster.

She pointed behind the altar, to the room from which light spilled. And Tanya. She backed out of the doorway, her hand pressed across her mouth as if to hold in another scream. As he rushed up behind her, she collided with Cooper. Then she pulled her hand away and screamed again.

He spun her around to face him. "It's okay," he assured her. "It's me."

Her green eyes, damp with tears, widened, and then she clutched at him, pressing against his chest. "Cooper! Thank God it's you!"

Her slight body trembled in his arms that automatically closed around her, pulling her even closer. She fit perfectly against him. But he was just comforting her, just making sure she was all right.

"What's wrong?" he asked. "Are you hurt?"

She shook her head, and her silky blond hair brushed against his throat. "No, no..."

He peered over her head into the room, and then he saw it. All the blood...

So much blood.

Despite his order to stay put, his mother joined them. "What's wrong—" she started to ask but gasped when she saw it, too.

"Call 911," Cooper said, thrusting his phone at her.

Then he stepped inside the room to look for the body. With that much blood, there had to be a body...

A dead one.

Chapter Two

"There is no body…"

Cooper's words drifted to Tanya through a thick haze of shock. He wasn't speaking to her, though; he hadn't since he'd asked if she was hurt. Of course he had been busy—searching the church and the surrounding grounds as well as talking to his family and the police officers who had arrived to investigate the scene of the crime.

The police had spoken to her. A somber-faced male officer had asked countless questions and not one of them had been if she was okay. Mrs. Payne had shooed off the man a while ago when she'd brought Tanya the cup of tea that was cooling in her hands. What the older woman had told the officer was right—Tanya had no idea what had happened. She'd only turned on the light to find the blood. All that blood…

The smear she'd found on the wall stained her hands. That was why she hadn't lifted the cup. It was why the heat of the tea would never warm her. She had blood on her hands…

"So we don't know," Cooper continued, his dark head bent close to his brother's, "if we're looking at a homicide or abduction."

Was it Logan or Parker to whom he spoke? They were

identical twins. Whichever one it was asked, "*Why* would it be either?"

Cooper shrugged shoulders so broad that they tested the seams of his black leather jacket. Despite the blood and the fear, during that moment she'd clung to him, she'd felt safe—with his arms around her. Just as he hadn't talked to her, he hadn't touched her since then either. Maybe that was why she felt so cold that she trembled.

"This is Stephen we're talking about," Cooper's brother persisted. "He was everyone's friend in high school. Did he change that much?"

"No," Tanya replied. "He's still everyone's friend." Her best friend. Where was he? And what had happened to him?

"Then maybe this isn't what it looks like," the twin replied.

"It looks like a crime scene," Cooper said. Yellow tape cordoned off the groom's quarters that police techs had photographed and processed for prints and whatever other evidence they'd found. "There's a lot of blood. The signs of a struggle. It's obvious somebody was dragged down the aisle."

That was why the runner had been bunched. Like the walls of the groom's quarters, it had also been stained with blood. While she'd been in the bride's room, some-one had attacked her groom and dragged him from the church. How hadn't she or Mrs. Payne heard any of the struggle?

Tanya had been in the bride's room, deciding that she did not want to be a bride. Mrs. Payne had been down-stairs in her office talking with the reverend. Unable to have a rehearsal without a groom, the minister had left after talking to the police.

"What the hell did you do?" the maid of honor, Tanya's

sister, shouted. She ran down the aisle toward the front of the church where Tanya sat in the pew near where the Payne brothers stood. But Rochelle didn't make it very far before she tripped over the rumpled runner.

Tanya's only other bridesmaid, who was also Cooper's sister, rushed up behind her and helped her to her unsteady feet. "Rochelle, let me get you some more coffee…"

"I don't need coffee!" Tanya's little sister shouted, her words only slightly slurred. "I need to know what she did with Stephen!"

"What *I* did with him?" Tanya asked. She set the teacup on the pew and rose up to meet her sister as Rochelle finally made it down the aisle.

"You don't care about him at all," Rochelle accused. "You've just been using him to get Grandfather's money. That's all you care about!" She vaulted herself at Tanya, knocking her to the ground.

The shock finally wore off—leaving Tanya able to register the pain. She felt the hardness of the floor beneath her back and the weight of her sister, who, despite the fact she was younger, was quite a bit taller and heavier. She could barely breathe with her on top of her. And she felt the sharp sting of her sister's slap. She had no right to fight back—not when everything Rochelle said was probably true.

But this was not the time or the place for Rochelle to throw one of her temper tantrums. Tanya had been trying to hold herself together for so long that she finally snapped under the emotional and physical pressure. "Grow up, you brat," she yelled. Using probably more strength than necessary, she shoved her sister back.

Rochelle didn't stay off. As Tanya stood up, her sister launched herself at her again. But this time strong hands caught Tanya before she hit the ground. With an arm wrapped around her waist, Cooper lifted her nearly off her feet.

The other bridesmaid, Nikki Payne, caught Rochelle, and tried to control her swinging hands and flailing feet. For her efforts, she took a hit to her face.

"Whatever happened to Stephen is your fault," Rochelle accused. "It's all your fault!"

Another stinging blow connected, bringing tears to Tanya's eyes. But the tears weren't from physical pain. Rochelle's verbal assault had hit her harder than her slap. Because she was right.

Whatever had happened to Stephen was all Tanya's fault. She literally had his blood on her hands.

"Aren't you glad you had brothers?" Cooper asked his sister as she rubbed her fingertips along the scratch on her cheek and winced. Nikki had somehow subdued her friend while Cooper had carried Tanya out of her reach. When Rochelle had been swinging, Tanya had barely defended herself from her younger sister's attack. Maybe she was in shock over having found Stephen's blood in the groom's quarters.

"Yeah," Nikki agreed. "You guys just punched each other. It was more civilized."

"We never punched you," he said.

"No," she agreed with a heavy sigh, almost as if she was disappointed that they hadn't. As the youngest and the only girl with three older brothers, she had often been left out of their roughhousing because they hadn't wanted to hurt her.

Tanya and her sister didn't have that relationship. Rochelle had definitely wanted to hurt her. How badly, though?

He could understand Rochelle being resentful of her

sister. Tanya was far more beautiful—with more delicate features and blonder hair and a thinner figure than her sister. But how deep was that resentment?

"Why'd you bring her here?" Cooper asked. At least he hoped Nikki had been the driver.

"She's Tanya's maid of honor," she replied. "I've been looking for her all night to make sure she got to the rehearsal."

"Mom put you to work, too?"

She sighed. "Enlisted me as part of the wedding party. I think she suspected there'd be a problem with Rochelle, and she and I have known each other since high school."

"You did subdue her." So much so that the woman sat quietly in a pew now, tears streaming down her flushed face. She seemed more distraught over the groom's disappearance than the bride was.

"Please point that out to Logan," Nikki beseeched him. Their eldest brother was on the other side of the heavy oak doors, talking on his cell phone in the vestibule. She shot him a glare through the windows at the back of the chapel. "He keeps me tied to a desk. He refuses to let me do an actual physical protection assignment."

Cooper bit his tongue before he verbally agreed with Logan. Nikki was so petite and fragile looking—just like their mother with her copper-colored hair and big brown eyes. But she had handled herself remarkably well with the taller and heavier Chesterfield sister. He touched her scratched cheek, making her wince again.

"Hey, I didn't want to hurt her," Nikki explained. "Or I would have taken her down faster. She's a friend, though…" Then she reached out and squeezed his arm. "I'm sorry about Stephen. Do you have any idea what happened?"

"We don't know anything for certain. There's a hell

of a lot of blood in the groom's quarters. But until the crime lab does a DNA test, we don't even know for certain that it's his." Except if it wasn't, where the hell was he, then? If there wasn't all that blood, Cooper might have believed his friend had just gotten a case of cold feet. He might have believed that if Stephen was marrying any woman but Tanya.

"Mom confirmed he was the only one in the room," Nikki said.

"Where was his best man?" Cooper asked.

Nikki lifted a reddish brow. "Where was *he?*" she asked, obviously referring to him.

"I told him I couldn't do it," Cooper reminded his little sister.

"Why not?"

"Why?" Cooper asked. "Why did he even ask me? We haven't seen each other in years."

"He showed up at the house to see you every time you were home on leave," Nikki said. "He stayed in touch."

But they'd both been busy. The letters few and far between and Cooper's visits home even more infrequent. He shrugged. "I just thought it was weird that he didn't have a closer friend he wanted to stand up there with him."

And weirder that he wanted Cooper. They had been good friends in high school—so good that Stephen must have realized how Cooper had really felt about Tanya. Had he wanted to rub his face in the fact he'd gotten the girl Cooper had wanted? And if so, then they hadn't really been that good of friends.

But Cooper still cared about him—still wanted him safe—which he probably would have been had Cooper actually been his best man. Then Stephen wouldn't have been alone in the groom's quarters.

"There are a couple of guys who were planning on

standing up there with him," Nikki said. "A friend from his office and a cousin, but I recruited them to help me find Rochelle. We'd been searching all the bars in River City."

"How'd you know that's where she was?" Maybe Logan was underestimating their sister's potential as a security expert.

"She left me a drunk voice mail."

Cooper glanced over at the crying woman and sighed. "So interrogating her would probably be a waste of time until Mom gets more coffee in her."

"You don't need to interrogate her," Tanya said as she rejoined them with an ice pack pressed against the cheek her sister had viciously slapped.

Apparently his mother was prepared for every wedding emergency—even catfights between the bride and maid of honor. What was her plan to handle a missing groom?

"I can tell you whatever Rochelle can," Tanya said.

But would she be truthful with him? "You'll tell me why she thinks you're just using Stephen to get your inheritance?"

Nikki nudged his arm. "Easy. She's not a suspect."

Maybe she should have been. As he'd already noted, she wasn't nearly as upset as a madly in love bride should have been when her groom mysteriously and apparently violently disappeared. When Cooper had quietly, so she wouldn't overhear him, questioned her reaction earlier, his mother and brother had insisted she was in shock.

But her green eyes were clear now and direct as she replied, "I'm not using Stephen."

"What about the inheritance? Your grandfather died a decade ago—don't you already have your money?" But if she did, why pick his mom's place for her wedding?

The chapel was small and the reception hall in the basement was hardly elegant enough for a billionaire bride.

She shook her head.

"Not yet," another voice chimed in to answer for her. A burly gray-haired man joined them inside the church. With his muscular build and military haircut, he looked more like a cop, but Cooper recognized the lawyer, Arthur Gregory, who'd made countless house calls to the mausoleum. "Neither she nor Rochelle will inherit until they marry."

If Rochelle was right and her sister was just after her inheritance, wouldn't she have gotten married ten years ago? Wouldn't Rochelle have?

"He's trying to control us even after his death," Rochelle murmured. "Mean son of a—"

"Miss Chesterfield," the lawyer admonished her. "Your grandfather had only your best interests at heart."

"He had no heart," Rochelle retorted. "The only reason he wanted us married was because he didn't think a female had enough brains to handle the kind of money he was leaving to us." She uttered a derisive snort. "Like our father did such a great job. He blew through all that money Grandfather gave him to divorce Mom and take off."

Cooper had never known what had happened to Tanya's father. She had always avoided talking about him. He'd been sensitive to that since he'd never wanted to talk about how he had lost his dad either.

"Mr. Gregory, is there a way around the will?" Tanya asked the lawyer.

Her sister gasped. "We don't even know what's happened to Stephen and all you care about is the money?"

"I care about him," Tanya said. "That's why I need the

money. In case this is a kidnapping, I'll need it to pay the ransom to get him back."

Arthur Gregory sighed. "There is no way to inherit that money unless you're married, Miss Chesterfield. And as you know, you only have a few more days…"

Tanya flinched as if the lawyer had slapped her, too.

"Why only a few more days?" Cooper asked.

"If she doesn't marry before she turns thirty, she forfeits her half of the inheritance," Rochelle replied. "Then I'll get it all when I marry."

The young woman must have been too drunk yet to realize that she'd just announced her motive for getting rid of her sister's groom. But if she was behind Stephen's disappearance, why was she so distraught over it?

"I need that money," Tanya repeated, "in case there's a ransom demand…"

If Stephen was alive…

But if he wasn't, why wouldn't his body have been left in the room? Someone had taken him for a reason. And what better reason than money?

"The only way you can access your funds is to marry," the lawyer insisted.

"Then she'll have to marry," Cooper's mother said as she joined them inside the church. She carried a tray with cups on it—probably filled with coffee, judging by the rich aroma wafting from the tray.

Rochelle seemed to have already sobered up. But Cooper was tempted to reach for a cup. He suspected it was going to be a long night.

"But if Stephen's been kidnapped, we won't get him back until I've paid for his return," Tanya pointed out.

"So you'll marry someone else," the wedding planner matter-of-factly replied as if it were easy to exchange one groom for another.

"Who?" Cooper asked.

His mother turned to him, her eyes wide with surprise that he hadn't already figured it out. "You, of course."

Cooper had had no intention of attending this wedding, let alone participating in it. He hadn't wanted to be the best man...and he sure as hell wasn't going to be the groom.

Chapter Three

Tanya's heart stung with rejection. She hadn't had to hear his words to know that Cooper had no intention of becoming her husband—for any reason. When his mother had suggested it, he had looked more horrified than he had when he'd seen the blood in the groom's quarters.

But she could hear his words now. He didn't know that, though. His family had gone into the bride's room for a private discussion. Tanya hadn't intended to invade their privacy, but she'd left her purse in that room along with her dress. And she really wanted to leave.

She couldn't stay here any longer—not with that crime scene tape draped across the entrance to the groom's quarters. Not with Stephen's blood on her hands...

And not with Cooper's words ringing in her ears.

"There is no way in hell that I am marrying Tanya Chesterfield!"

"Cooper!" his mother admonished him as if he were a little boy who'd cussed in church.

"Mom!" he retorted. "You've been pushing me to attend this wedding since you first talked to Tanya about planning it—either as a guest or the best man. You are not pushing me to the altar as her groom."

She could have opened the door; it was the bride's room, after all. But she was no longer going to be a bride.

Her groom was missing and the only other man she would want to take his place had flat-out refused. Not that she really wanted Cooper as her groom or anything else...

She turned away from the door. Instead of revealing that she'd been eavesdropping, she would leave her purse and just walk home. Her apartment was on the third floor of a home in the same area of town as Mrs. Payne's Little White Wedding Chapel, so it wasn't far. And her landlord on the ground floor had a spare key to her place.

But as soon as she stepped outside the heavy oak doors, the night air chilled her blood and she shivered. Stephen was out here somewhere. With whoever had hurt him.

Why hurt Stephen? Why not just hurt her as the threats she'd been receiving for the past ten years had promised?

As she descended the steep stairs to the sidewalk, she shivered again and wished she would have agreed to ride along with Nikki and Rochelle. But she hadn't wanted to be in the same room—let alone the same car—with her sister. Since Rochelle was six years younger than she was, they had never been particularly close, but they had gotten along well enough. Until Tanya had become officially engaged...

She should have asked someone else to be her maid of honor. But she'd thought that maybe including Rochelle would bring her around, would bring them closer.

Instead, they were more at odds than they had ever been. At least the cold air felt good on Tanya's still-stinging cheek. She lifted her face to the breeze and let it caress her skin. Maybe walking home wouldn't be so bad after all.

It was dark. But streetlamps, the ones not covered with overhanging branches, illuminated the sidewalk. Despite the light, she tripped over a crack and remembered the velvet runner. Stephen had been dragged down the aisle so that he couldn't become her groom.

Cooper Payne would have to be dragged down the aisle in order to become her groom. It wasn't going to happen. She was going to lose her inheritance, but far worse, she was going to lose her friend.

A car drove slowly past her, its windows tinted so she couldn't see inside it. Whoever the driver was, he or she was traveling well below the speed limit—nearly at the speed with which Tanya was walking. She shivered again—this time with a sense of foreboding instead of from the cold.

And she remembered those threats—all those promises that she would lose her life before she would ever inherit her money. Had Stephen's disappearance just been a diversion, a way to distract her from protecting herself?

Not only had she left her keys in her purse, but she'd left her cell phone, rape whistle, inhaler, EpiPen and pepper spray, too.

"COME ON," COOPER urged his brother. "Tell her it's a crazy idea."

But Logan didn't even glance at their mother. He just continued to stare at him, as if considering.

"It's crazy," Coop insisted.

His mother glared at him. "I thought the Marines would teach you some respect."

"I didn't call *you* crazy," he pointed out. "Just your idea…" It was ridiculous. Tanya had obviously thought it so ridiculous that she hadn't said a thing, as if she'd gone back into shock. So they'd just left her sitting there in the church—alone—as Stephen had been in that now-blood-spattered room. A frisson of unease trickled down his spine like a drop of ice water.

Tanya had been alone in this room earlier, but she'd been left unharmed. Probably so she could pay the ransom to recover her groom. She would be safe out there—especially as there had been an officer or two hanging around yet to finish processing the crime scene.

"But it's not crazy," Logan said. "It's brilliant."

"Br-brilliant?" Cooper choked on the word and coughed.

And his mother slapped his shoulder. "Of course it is." But she seemed surprised, too, that her oldest would agree with her. She had always said that although Logan was a twin, he definitely had a mind of his own.

"Can't you see that?" Logan asked with concern, as if Cooper was more dim-witted than he'd remembered.

So Cooper mentally stepped back, as he often had had to during his deployments, and he assessed the situation. "Stephen's missing. Maybe he just got cold feet." Even as he said it, he doubted his words. The Stephen he'd known had been an honorable guy; he wouldn't have just run away—especially not from Tanya.

Cooper had been the only man he knew of who had run from her—back when they'd been kids and his new feelings for his friend had overwhelmed him and also because her grandfather had made him see that it would never work out between them. It didn't matter that the old man was dead now; Benedict Bradford was still right.

"Then why all the blood?" Logan persisted.

Cooper visualized the crime scene that may not have been a crime scene at all. There was a small hammered-copper sink in the room with a mirror above it. He could have been shaving his neck and slipped with the blade, nicking his artery. "Maybe he accidentally hurt himself."

But there had been no razor or anything else sharp left at the scene…

"If that was the case, he would have gotten help," Logan pointed out. "Mom and Tanya and even Reverend James were all in the building, too."

"But we didn't hear anything," his mother reminded him.

Desperate to believe that Stephen would return, Cooper persisted in his argument, "Maybe, when you guys didn't hear him calling, he left and got help somewhere else."

"His car is still in the lot," his mother pointed out.

"He could have called a damn cab," Cooper remarked.

"But then he would have showed up at an E.R. by now," Logan argued. "Parker and a team of Payne employees are checking every emergency room and med station, and Stephen hasn't shown up anywhere yet."

Cooper begrudgingly admitted, "Maybe he has been abducted."

"Why?" Logan fired the question at him even though the answer was obvious.

Conceding his loss of this argument, he groaned before replying, "For Tanya's money."

"Which she can't access until she's married," his mother chimed in again. "She won't be able to pay the ransom when the demands are made."

His mother was right. Unfortunately.

But there was another possibility, one he hated to even voice, but he forced out the words, "He could be dead."

Cooper's guts tightened with guilt at the horrific thought. If only he'd agreed to be the damn best man, he would have been in that room with him, he could have protected him. Hell, if he hadn't dragged his feet getting to the church…

As if he'd read his mind, Logan reassuringly gripped his shoulder. "You don't know that…"

No, he didn't know if Stephen was dead, but he knew that he could have helped—had he been at the church in time.

"Neither do you," Cooper said, which probably infuriated Logan since his eldest brother thought he knew everything.

"Then where's his body?" Logan asked. "Why would his killer take it with him? Why wouldn't he have just left it in the room?"

Cooper wasn't the one with the law enforcement background. "You were the cop." A detective actually and a greatly decorated one, just as their father had been a police officer. "You know it's harder to press murder charges, let alone convict, without a body."

"The crime scene techs said that it looked like a lot of blood because of the spray, but there wasn't enough for someone to have bled to death," Logan reminded him.

"Yet." But if he was injured and didn't get help... "We should be out there looking for him, not wasting our time with this crazy discussion."

"Parker and his team aren't just checking hospitals and med centers. They're looking for him everywhere," Logan reminded him. "They've checked his place, his work—all of his usual hangouts."

"And they haven't found him," Cooper said. "We need to search harder and even then we may not find him alive." Or at all.

How many people had gone missing to never be seen again? He'd personally known a few—in Afghanistan.

"There's still time to help him," his mother insisted. Despite all she'd lost when her husband had died, she still remained an optimist. "But in case there is a ransom demand, Tanya will need her inheritance to pay it."

"So *someone* needs to marry her," Logan said.

His mother patted Cooper's arm again but more gently this time. "It's all right," she said as if he were a child she was reassuring about going to the dentist. "If you don't want to do it, Parker can."

Parker, the playboy, marrying Tanya? His gut churned at the thought—it was even crazier than *him* marrying her. In fact, him marrying her actually made the most sense since they knew each other, since he had actually kissed the bride before. Besides, it was his fault that Stephen had disappeared. If only he'd been in the groom's quarters before Stephen had been taken...

Rejecting his mother's suggestion, he shook his head. "I'll do it."

His mother clapped her hands together. "Great. I will call a certain judge I know to rush a new marriage certificate, and we'll proceed with the wedding tomorrow, just as we'd planned."

He was getting married *tomorrow?* Panic gripped him, squeezing his chest so tightly that he couldn't draw a deep breath.

"Maybe someone should tell the bride that," Logan suggested with a slight grin.

His mother gestured toward a leather purse sitting on the floor beneath a hanging garment bag. "She wouldn't have left without that, so she must still be here."

But she wasn't. As they had for Stephen, they searched the entire church. But they didn't find her.

Only the blood...

It was dried. It was old. It wasn't hers.

There was no fresh blood. No signs of a new struggle. No Tanya.

"Where could she have gone?" Cooper asked, and now he was panicking for another reason than getting married tomorrow. He was panicking that he might not be able to get married because the bride had disappeared like the original groom.

"Maybe she decided to walk home," his mother suggested.

The police officer who had been watching the parking lot in case Stephen returned for his car had mentioned seeing her leave the church.

"You actually think she could walk to the estate?" Cooper asked, shaking his head. "No way."

The mausoleum was on the other side of the very sprawling city. The distance between the church and the estate was more of a marathon than an evening stroll. But the officer hadn't seen a cab.

"She lives just a couple of blocks over," his mother said. "She rents a third-floor apartment."

"An *apartment?*" he asked, even more confused. She was a billionaire's granddaughter and she *rented?*

"She hasn't inherited yet," his mother reminded him, "and on her salary as a social worker, she can't afford to buy her own house."

So why hadn't she married sooner? Why wait until within days of forfeiting her inheritance? Despite having known Tanya for years, he really had no idea who she was. Of course, he had been gone for most of those years.

Now he had no idea where she was...

He grabbed her purse from his mom and opened it up. Her cell phone was inside—along with an inhaler, an EpiPen, a can of pepper spray and a shiny whistle. Given some of the danger social workers confronted, she should have carried a gun, too. He flipped open her wallet to read the address on her driver's license. The picture distracted him for a minute. Even on the tiny snapshot, she was beautiful—her blond hair shining like gold and her green eyes sparkling as she smiled brightly.

That was what had been so different about her to-night. The fear. The anxiety. She wasn't the Tanya he remembered because she was a woman now, not a care-free teenager.

"Look at that," Logan said with a slight grin. "Not even married yet and already carrying her purse." That was the way their family had always handled strife and loss—with wisecracking.

But Cooper didn't have time for it now, not with Tanya missing. He was going to follow her route from the church to her apartment and find her—hopefully alive.

"Shut up," he said. "And keep an eye on Mom."

She shouldn't be alone in a building where someone had already been abducted, just as Tanya should have never been left alone. Once he was her husband, Cooper would make damn sure that she stayed safe. But now he wondered if she would even make it to the altar.

THE CAR WITH the darkly tinted windows circled the block again like a cat stalking a bird. Was the driver waiting for Tanya to step off the sidewalk? She needed to cross the street if she intended to head home.

But if she headed home, wouldn't she be leading the driver right to her door? But given the threats she'd received through the mail, her stalker already knew where she lived. So if the driver was her stalker, he already knew where she was going.

She needed to turn back to the church. But if the others had left…

Mrs. Payne would have locked up, locking Tanya's purse and phone inside the bride's room. But she hadn't been gone that long, surely someone might have stayed behind.

Cooper?

She wasn't certain she wanted to see him, knowing how he felt about the thought of becoming her husband for just a few days—until she inherited. Once the money was hers, she could divorce him. Maybe he didn't know that; maybe she should have explained. But she hadn't wanted to force him to do something he clearly did not want to do.

They had once been friends. Good friends. Along with Stephen, they had been like the Three Musketeers— studying and hanging out together. But now Cooper acted like a stranger. Had his deployments overseas changed him that much?

Or was she the one who had changed? She used to want to have nothing to do with her grandfather's money, but then she had nearly married to inherit it. Had gone so far as to plan a wedding to a man she loved but wasn't in love with…

Tanya shivered at the cold wind and the eerie sensation that someone was hiding in the darkness, watching her. Coming for her. But then it wasn't just a sensation. It was a certainty.

She blew out a ragged breath as the car circled again, driving even more slowly along the street. As long as she stayed on the sidewalk, maybe she would stay safe. But then the car tires squealed as the driver jerked the steering wheel. Sparks flew from beneath the front bumper as it scraped over concrete as the car jumped the curb and headed right for her.

She screamed, her legs burning as she ran.

But it didn't matter how fast she ran or how loud she yelled, she couldn't outrun a motor vehicle. She hadn't been able to save Stephen, and now she wouldn't be able to save herself.

Chapter Four

For the second time that night, Tanya's scream pierced the air and Cooper's heart. The car's lights illuminated her. Her eyes were wide and her face pale with terror. He hurried to catch up but she was ahead of him, the car between them.

"Run!" he yelled, urging her to move as the car barreled down on her where she ran across the front yards of a row of houses. As a kid she hadn't been able to run very far or very fast because her asthma would act up. Hopefully, she'd outgrown that.

Cooper had already drawn his weapon. But if he shot at the driver, the bullet might pass through the windshield and hit Tanya before the front bumper of the car could. So he aimed at the tires and quickly squeezed the trigger.

One back tire popped, deflating fast so that it shredded and slapped against the rim. But despite the flat, the car continued forward—straight toward Tanya.

Still running, Tanya veered between two houses. But the houses weren't so far apart that the car couldn't follow her.

Cooper shot out the other back tire and the car swerved, careening across a lawn. It scraped against a tree and proceeded to the street, cutting off another vehicle that blared its horn. Sparks flew from the rims riding the asphalt, but the car didn't stop. Yet. Eventually it would have to, though, so Cooper figured he might be able to catch up to it on foot.

But he had a greater concern. "Tanya!"

He ran across the yards, stumbling over the deep ruts that the car had torn in the muddy spring lawn. Then he veered between the two houses as she had. Lights flickered on inside those houses, brightening a couple of the dark windows. They must have heard either the car or his yelling. His throat burned from the force of his shouts. "Tanya!"

He nearly stumbled over her where she lay sprawled across the ground. The light from the houses cast only a faint glow into the backyards, so he could barely see her. He holstered his gun and then dropped to his knees beside her. His hands shook as he reached for her.

Despite his efforts to stop it, had the car struck her anyway? Had it run over her once it had knocked her down? He couldn't tell if she was conscious or not, if she was alive or dead. Her hair had fallen across her face, the strands tangled. He brushed it back as he slid his hand down her throat, checking for a pulse. Thankfully, she started breathing, but laboriously, the breaths rattling in her chest.

Obviously she hadn't outgrown her asthma and all the running had brought on an attack. She opened her eyes, the light glinting in them.

"Are you okay?" he asked. "Do you need your inhaler?" He'd left it in her purse back at the church, though.

She sucked in a shuddery breath and then choked and gasped.

Cooper wanted to pick her up and cradle her in his arms, but he didn't dare move her if she was hurt. "Did the car hit you?"

Bracing her palms on the ground, she began pushing herself up. But Cooper caught her shoulders, steadying her. "Don't move. If you're hurt—"

"I'm not hurt," she said as she tried to control her breathing. "I just fell."

Maybe she'd only been out of breath from running as fast as she'd had to so the car wouldn't have run her over. "Are you sure?"

"I'm not hurt," she repeated. "Because of you…" Then she threw her arms around his neck and clung to him as she had when he'd first arrived at the church. "Thank you!"

But Cooper couldn't accept her gratitude—not with the guilt plaguing him. It wasn't just guilt that had his heart racing, though. It was fear. And probably her closeness. With every breath he took, he breathed her in; she smelled like flowers and grass. And the grass reminded him that she could have been killed. He grabbed her shoulders and pulled her away from him. "What were you thinking to leave the church on your own?"

She tensed. "I was thinking I wanted to get the hell out of there."

Was that his fault for not immediately agreeing to his mother's suggestion that he marry her? Had he hurt her pride?

"Then why didn't you leave with Nikki when she took your sister home?" he asked.

She uttered a mirthless chuckle. "Do you really think I would have been any safer with my sister?"

"She wouldn't have tried to run you over with a car," he pointed out as he helped her to her feet.

She stumbled as if her legs were still shaky. But instead of leaning on him again, she steadied herself. "No," she agreed, "but she might have tried to shove me out of one."

He couldn't argue that, not after the way Rochelle had attacked her in the church.

"Cooper!" Logan called out to him as he ran between the houses and joined them in the backyard. "I couldn't catch the car."

He had forgotten that his brother had been right behind him when he'd left the church. His order for Logan to stay with their mom had been overruled—by their mother. She'd reminded them that the police officer was still in the parking lot and even if he wasn't, she could take care of herself. She was armed, and their father had taught her how to shoot very well.

Logan was huffing and puffing for breath. "I could barely keep up with you."

When Cooper had heard Tanya scream, he had taken off running. He reached for his cell phone now. "Did you call the police?"

"Called 'em," Logan said, which was confirmed with sirens whining in the distance. "Did you get a better look at the car than I did?"

"Long and dark," Cooper replied. "With the windows too darkly tinted to see inside."

"What about the plate?"

"There wasn't one."

This hadn't been some drunk driver whose car jumped the curb and veered into a yard. This near-miss hit-and-run had been planned.

Just to scare her or to kill her?

TANYA HELD HER breath, pressing down the fear that threatened to choke her. She stared up at the dark windows of her apartment, wishing she could see inside, but she stood on the sidewalk three floors below. Light flashed behind the arched window in the peak of the attic where she lived.

Was it the beam of a flashlight or the flash of gunfire? She gasped, and the breath she'd held escaped in a rush of fear.

"You shouldn't have let him go inside alone," she admonished his brother. "The driver of that car could be in there, waiting..." For her. And Cooper would step into the trap her stalker might have laid for her.

She should have had one of the police officers who'd taken the report for the near hit-and-run bring her home. They had offered a ride and protection. But the Payne brothers had assured the officers that they would make sure she stayed safe.

How? By putting themselves at risk?

Logan chuckled. "Cooper can handle himself and whoever he might encounter." His slight grin slipped into a frown that furrowed his brow. "He wouldn't have survived three deployments in Afghanistan if he couldn't."

But how many soldiers had survived war only to come home and die in an auto accident? Or some other freak crime—like a shooting? She kept her gaze trained on those third-floor windows and saw another flash of light.

Reaching out, she clutched Logan's arm. "I see something! Something's happening up there!"

Logan's gaze rose toward the third floor, too. "I don't see anything..."

But he must have been concerned, too, because he pulled out his cell phone. He pressed a button for what must have been a two-way feature and then he called out, "Cooper?"

Not even a crackle of static emanated from his phone, it remained dead.

She shuddered as the horrible thought occurred to her that Cooper might have been dead, too. She hadn't heard any shots, but some guns had silencers. She knew that from watching TV. The person who might have been waiting in her apartment could have had one.

She tugged on the sleeve of Logan's wool overcoat. "You need to go upstairs and check on him!"

"He needs to stay with you," a deep voice coming out of the darkness corrected her. "Like someone should have stayed with you at the church so you didn't go running off on your own."

She hadn't started running until the car had jumped the curb to chase her down. But she didn't bother pointing that out since the sharpness of his voice showed he was already angry with her.

And Logan was already asking, "Did you clear the apartment, Cooper?"

"No."

Logan snorted derisively. "Why not? It doesn't look that big."

The studio apartment had formerly been a ballroom, so it was bigger than it looked—with a bathroom tucked into a wide dormer. If the attic space didn't have issues with being too hot in the summer and too cold in the winter, the rent wouldn't have been affordable enough for her.

"I cleared it for intruders, but there were other threats," Cooper explained.

Logan tensed and held up his phone, his fingers ready to press buttons. "What do we need? Bomb squad?"

"If it was a bomb, I would have taken care of it," he assured his brother. "No, it was *literally* other threats." He passed his brother the desecrated engagement announcement.

While Tanya sucked in a breath of indignation that

Cooper had gone through her things, his brother released a ragged breath of relief.

But Cooper wasn't relaxed. His jaw was clenched so tightly that a muscle twitched in his cheek. He was obviously mad as hell, his dark gaze intense as he stared at Tanya.

She glared back at him. He was only supposed to make sure her place was safe. The thought of him going through her boxes and drawers and closets reminded her of all the things he might have found, like her weakness for silk and lace underwear.

"There are more of those," he told his brother. "Did you know about the threats?"

"No," Logan replied.

"Now you know," Cooper said. "Get on it. Check out her ex-boyfriends, her cases at work—"

Logan grinned. "Are you forgetting which one of us is the boss, little brother? I've been doing this for a while. I need to talk to the client first to get the names of those ex-boyfriends and difficult cases."

Cooper shook his head. "I'll do that."

If she were actually a client, she would rather talk to Logan. She could be more honest with him because she suspected he would be less judgmental. But she wasn't actually a client and needed to remind the protective Payne brothers of that. "I haven't hired—"

Cooper interrupted her as he spoke to his brother. "Tanya and I need to talk."

As if Logan, too, had forgotten he was the boss, he nodded his agreement. "I need to touch base with Parker…"

Probably to see if he had found Stephen. But if he had, he would have called. Even if he'd found him dead, he would have called. She shuddered now, so forcefully that she couldn't stop trembling.

"If you completely cleared her place, get her inside," Logan, as the boss again, ordered. "She's freezing. Or in shock…"

"Or getting pissed off that she's being ignored," Tanya suggested. "Yes," she continued, ignoring them as they had been ignoring her, "she's definitely pissed off."

Logan patted his brother's shoulder before heading toward his car parked at the curb. "Good luck. You may be the one needing protection now."

As if Tanya could take out a Marine, no matter how angry she was. And she actually wasn't as angry as she was scared. For Stephen. For herself. For Cooper…

"I won't hurt you," she assured him.

He uttered one of his brother's derisive snorts as if he didn't believe her. "Did you tell Stephen that, too?"

Her palm itched to slap him as her sister had slapped her. Her cheek throbbed at just the memory of that blow—or maybe because she'd hit it again when she'd done the nosedive running away from the car. Bristling with anger and with guilt over Stephen's disappearance, she said nothing as they climbed the stairs to her apartment.

Since he had the keys he'd gotten from her landlord, he unlocked the door and stepped inside first, as if checking again for an intruder. Then he flipped on the lights.

A banker's box had been knocked over, the contents spilled across the library table that also served as her dining table and desk. She gasped. "Someone was in here?"

He shook his head. "Not that I could tell."

"You did this?" He must have gone through her things in a hurry. Maybe he hadn't had time to look through her closet and drawers. She glanced around, but it appeared nothing else had been disturbed. So she focused again on the contents of the box. All those threats…

She had packed them away—hoping to forget them but not foolish enough to throw them all out.

"You haven't exactly been forthcoming with information," he bitterly reminded her. "If we're going to find Stephen, we need to know everything."

If…

She wasn't naive. She knew it was very likely that they would never find Stephen…either alive or dead. But she wasn't ready to face that possibility. She would have preferred Cooper offer assurances and promises. But she knew him better than that. He would never give her what she wanted from him—at least he hadn't when they were teenagers.

"There isn't much to tell you," she said, especially when it came to exes. "I haven't really dated much." Because of the threats. And maybe because of him, but she didn't want him to suspect that she'd hung on to an old crush. "I've been too busy with work."

"How long have you been a social worker?" he asked. "Since you graduated college? You must have handled a lot of cases."

She sighed as faces jumbled in her mind. "A lot," she agreed, "but none recently. At least not personally. I became a supervisor four years ago. I delegate now." Which meant giving too much work to too few employees.

"Now," he said. "But four years ago there must have been cases you handled that hadn't gone well."

She flinched, remembering the losses. The people she hadn't been able to help. If she had Grandfather's money, she could do so much more than she was able to do now. "Of course there were cases that went badly. Children I had to remove from neglectful or abusive parents." She shuddered at the painful memories. "But that was years ago…"

"Some people have a hard time forgiving the person they perceive tore their family apart," he said with a glance out toward the street. "Mom says Logan has never missed a parole hearing for the man who shot my father. He's determined to make sure that the guy never gets out of prison—at least not alive."

"What about you?" she asked. He had never talked about his father's death before, but back then it had been too recent and probably too painful for a teenage boy to process let alone express.

"What about me?" he asked as if his feelings didn't matter. "I haven't been here for any of the parole hearings." And maybe that was why he thought his feelings didn't matter—because he had been gone so long. He had left his family.

And her. But they'd only just been friends, high school friends who often drifted apart after graduation. She hadn't really meant anything to him. But she knew that his family had meant everything to him.

"If you had been here, would you have gone to those hearings?"

He shrugged. "I think it's best to leave the past in the past."

She and Stephen were his past.

"But most people don't feel that way," he continued. He passed her a legal pad and a pen. "Write down the names of the guys you've dated. And write down any cases you remember where someone might be holding a grudge against you."

"I really can't," she protested. "There are privacy laws I have to obey."

"What about Stephen?"

He was her best friend. And he was missing. If there was any chance of getting him back, her pride and her job could be damned. So she wrote down some names.

"He knew," she said, finally defending herself from his earlier comment. "Stephen knew about the threats."

Cooper sucked in a breath. "And he wanted to marry you anyway? He must love you a lot."

As a friend. But if she told Cooper that, he would think the same thing her sister did—that she was just using Stephen to get her inheritance.

"I love him a lot, too," she said. *But only as a friend.*

Cooper's jaw went rigid again, as if he was clenching it. He nodded. "Stephen's a good man. And a lawyer. Your grandfather would have approved."

Probably, but only until she'd given away all his ruthlessly earned money.

"We have to find him," she said. And she couldn't rely on an overworked police department. "I really can't afford Payne Protection—not until I get my inheritance. But I want to hire your family." They specialized in security, working mainly as bodyguards, but Logan and Parker were both former police officers. And Cooper was…Cooper. The kind of man who stopped a speeding car from barreling over a woman.

Had she even thanked him? She couldn't remember now; it had all been such a blur of terror and disbelief and then relief.

His brow furrowed with confusion. "We're already on the job. Why do you think I showed up at the church in the first place?"

She had been so upset over finding the blood in the empty groom's quarters that she hadn't given it much thought then. "I don't know…maybe you had changed your mind about being Stephen's best man."

But that wasn't the case. She already knew that from when she'd eavesdropped outside the bride's room. He had been pretty clear that he'd wanted no part of his mother's manipulations. Why had the wedding planner been so intent on getting Cooper to attend the ceremony? It wasn't as if he would have stood up and protested their union—at least not to claim her as his bride. Definitely not to claim her as his bride…

"I wish I had agreed to be his best man," Cooper admitted. "Then I would have been there…"

Her heart lurched. "And you could have been hurt, too." Or worse…

Just as his brother had said while they'd waited for him to make sure her apartment was safe, he reminded her, "I can take care of myself."

Cooper wouldn't have gone anywhere willingly. Not that Stephen had. *Poor Stephen…*

"And I can take care of you, too," he said. "I'll keep you safe."

He had already proven that—when he'd stopped a speeding car.

"That's why I showed up at the church," he said. He scooped up some of the shriveled petals that had fallen from the black roses. "Mom took the delivery of these and knew something was wrong."

"I'm sorry I brought your mother into this," she said, suspecting that could have been the reason for some of his anger earlier. "I thought those threats were empty. I didn't believe anyone would actually act on them." Or she would have never agreed to marry her best friend. "I've been getting them for years…"

"How many years?" he asked.

She sighed and replied, "Ten years."

"Around the time your grandfather died?"

Cooper remembered when Grandfather had died? He had been deployed at the time; he must have had greater concerns on his mind than her loss—such as it had been. Benedict Bradford had never been a very warm or loving man.

"Yes," she replied. "I didn't get them all that often—only when I started seriously seeing someone."

"Someone sure didn't want you collecting your inheritance," he mused, staring down at the box of threats.

She sighed again. "They got what they wanted." And they'd gotten Stephen, too. Would they give him back… without the money?

Her stomach churned with dread and worry that they wouldn't, that she might never see her dear friend again. And the tears she'd been fighting back for so long rushed up with such force that they burst out. She couldn't hold back the sobs while tears streamed from her eyes.

Strong arms wrapped around her, pulling her close. And a big hand gently patted her hair. "No, they haven't gotten what they wanted."

She shook her head, and his fingers slipped through her hair and skimmed down her neck. A rush of heat stemmed her tears. "There're only a few days before my thirtieth birthday. I hope we find Stephen before then." She doubted that they would, though. "But even if we do, I can't put him at risk again. I can't marry Stephen."

"You're not going to marry Stephen," he agreed.

Because her groom was missing…

What if he was already dead? Her heart beat heavily with anguish. And more tears trickled out, sliding down her cheeks.

Cooper wiped them away with his thumbs. "You're going to marry me."

Her heart rate quickened to a frantic pace. She gazed up at him in disbelief. "What? You didn't agree to that."

"I changed my mind," he said. "I'm going to be your groom. You're still getting married tomorrow."

Maybe Rochelle's slaps had hit her hard enough to addle her brain. She couldn't understand what he was saying. What he meant...

Maybe it was because he was too close, his arms around her—his heart pounding hard against hers. And he was leaning down, his head so close that she could see tiny black flecks in the bright blue of his eyes. She could see the shadow of his lashes on his cheeks and the stubble that was already darkening his jaw.

She wanted to reach up and run her fingers over that stubble, up his chin to his lips. All these years later she still remembered how they felt—silky but firm. But she didn't want to just touch his lips; she wanted to kiss them. The urge was so great that she rose on tiptoe.

But before she could close the slight distance between their mouths, she jerked out of his arms. She couldn't be having these thoughts—these desires for Cooper. She needed air to clear her head, so she moved toward the big arched window that looked out onto the street below. But before she could lift the bottom pane, the glass shattered.

Gunshots echoed.

And she was falling to the ground, pushed down as more gunshots rang out. Pain radiated throughout her body and she wondered if it was already too late.

Would she live to see her wedding day?

Chapter Five

Glass showered down over them, nicking Cooper's face and the back of his neck. Too bad he still had his military brush cut. Blood trickled from his nape over his throat.

He needed to jump up and return gunfire. But that would mean leaving Tanya unprotected. And he couldn't do that. Again. He covered her body with his, pressing her into the hardwood floor.

Since the shooter on the street wouldn't be able to hear them, he leaned his face close to her ear and whispered, "Are you okay?"

She shivered, trembling beneath him. But she didn't speak. Maybe *she* was worried that the shooter could hear them.

But the gunfire had stopped. Maybe the assailant was just reloading. Or maybe he had gone.

"Tanya, are you okay?" he asked again.

Her breath shuddered out in a ragged sigh. She must have been holding it, and she murmured, "I think so..."

But he heard the doubt in her voice and eased up so she could roll over and face him. "Were you hit?" he asked. He ran his hands down her sides, checking for wounds. Just for wounds...

But he found soft curves and lean muscles instead. Heat tingled in his hands and in other parts of his body. A few minutes ago, he'd thought she was going to kiss him. Their mouths had been only a breath apart, but maybe that was because he'd leaned down—because he'd wanted to kiss her so badly his gut had clenched.

The woman got to him as no one else ever had. And that made her dangerous—almost as dangerous as the shooter.

She squirmed beneath him. Apparently she was still as ticklish as when they'd been kids. He used to tickle her then—just as an excuse to touch her.

But he'd had a reason to touch her this time. "Are you hurt?" he asked again.

When his hand skimmed over her rib cage, she sucked in a breath. "Just sore," she murmured, "from my fall."

She'd fallen twice. Once in the church when her sister had attacked her and again when the car had nearly run her down. Actually, three times since he'd shoved her to the floor—which was unyielding hardwood.

He wasn't doing the greatest job protecting her. Maybe Logan had been right and he wasn't ready yet for a field job. But he couldn't imagine anyone else protecting her. Or marrying her.

She lifted her hand and skimmed her fingers over his throat, making his pulse leap even more wildly. And her eyes widened with shock and horror. "You're bleeding! You've been hit! We need to call an ambulance!"

He brushed away the trickle of blood. "It's just a scratch from the flying glass."

He brushed some of those glass fragments from her silky blond hair and his fingertips tingled. He didn't even notice the bite of the glass. All he noticed was the fresh flowery scent of her and the soft feel of her. She was so close. He only needed to lean down a few inches to close the distance between them and press his lips to hers.

"I'm fine," he assured her. But he wasn't. He was tempted to kiss his best friend's bride while the man was missing. But hell, Cooper was the one who was going to marry her. Tomorrow. He drew in a deep breath to steady his racing pulse. "We should call the police."

"He's gone?" she asked hopefully.

He wasn't certain about that…even though he had heard the squeal of tires as a car sped away.

"We still need to call to report the shooting." There could be shell casings recovered. Witnesses questioned that might be able to identify the shooter. He reached for his cell phone.

And then he heard the footsteps, the stairs creaking beneath the weight of the person stealthily climbing up to Tanya's apartment. Maybe the shooter hadn't sped off in the car with the squealing tires. Maybe he had come upstairs to make sure he'd killed his intended victim.

Cooper drew his weapon from the holster on his belt. He pointed the barrel at the door as he scrambled to his feet and helped up Tanya. He shoved her toward the only other room in the studio apartment. The bathroom.

"Get in the tub," he ordered her in an urgent whisper. Where he'd been, grenades were routinely tossed in houses. Or machine-gun fire that cut through walls like scissors through paper. "And stay down."

He didn't know if she did as he told her because she closed that door. And another opened, slowly, the old hinges creaking in protest. His finger twitched on the trigger as he prepared to pull it, especially as the first thing that entered the apartment was the barrel of a gun.

He waited to get a target before he took his shot. But just as he was about to squeeze the trigger, the intruder stepped from the shadows and revealed himself.

"Damn it, Logan!" he cursed his brother. "I almost shot you!"

Logan holstered his gun and gestured toward the broken window. "Looks like you got a little trigger-happy already."

Cooper begrudgingly admitted, "I didn't fire my weapon." Then he pointed toward the holes in the drywall ceiling. "The shooter was down on the street."

Which had probably saved Tanya's life and his, because the trajectory of the bullets had sent them tunneling into the ceiling instead of into their bodies.

Sirens blared and blue and red lights flashed, refracting off all the broken glass. "And now the police are down there," Logan pointed out with a slight sigh of relief.

Either the landlord or a neighbor must have called them. Cooper hadn't had the chance to dial yet. He'd been too distracted. Tanya had distracted him.

"Why are *you* here?" he asked his older brother, who was also now his boss. "You checking up on me?" He couldn't blame him if he was. His first assignment with Payne Protection and he was already blowing it. First, he'd lost Stephen, and he'd nearly lost Tanya more than once.

"You said you were going to get some information for me," Logan reminded him. "Tanya's list of difficult cases and exes."

"What? Were you waiting in the car for it?" Cooper asked—almost hopefully. Because if his brother had been just outside, he would have seen something.

Logan shook his head. "No. I went back to the church to check on Mom and she ordered me back here."

"She ordered you?" Cooper teased. "I thought you were the boss."

Logan chuckled. "Doesn't matter who's listed as CEO, Mom will always be the *boss*."

"She sent you back for the list?" Maybe their mother was running Payne Protection, too.

"She sent me back for Tanya."

More footsteps sounded on the staircase. "That's probably the police."

"Once you two give your report, I need to take Tanya with me," Logan said.

"So Mom doesn't trust me to protect her?" He flinched at the pang of regret. She had always had more faith in her oldest son than her youngest.

Logan chuckled again. "No. It's all about tradition or superstition…"

"What is?" Cooper asked as his head began to pound with confusion and exhaustion. He'd endured tours of duty that had been less dangerous and stressful than this night. "What are you talking about?"

"Mom doesn't want you to spend the night before your wedding with your bride."

Usually Tanya sank into her claw-foot tub with a sigh of relief as the hot water eased the tension from her body. Her tub would never again relieve her stress because she had never been as scared as she was crouched down beneath the rim.

Someone was obviously determined that Tanya wouldn't live to see her wedding day. With Cooper agreeing to take Stephen's place as her groom, the wedding could take place as scheduled—the next day. So Tanya would have to die tonight.

Would Cooper die with her? Had he already? She'd heard no shots.

But then the bathroom door opened to men with guns.

But they were uniformed police officers. Cooper hadn't come for her. She had heard no shots—only the rumble of male voices. Had he been hurt worse than he'd claimed? Had he really been bleeding from just a scratch?

The heat flushed her face; she was embarrassed that strangers had found her hiding in her bathtub. At least she was fully clothed, though.

"Are you okay, ma'am?" a young officer asked as he helped her step over the porcelain rim.

Her legs trembled slightly, in reaction from all she'd endured that day and in exhaustion. "I'm fine," she said. "Is Mr. Payne all right?"

"Which Mr. Payne?" he asked.

When she stepped out of the bathroom, she found the brothers talking to another officer.

"This is the third report we've had to file for you guys tonight," the older policeman said with a grunt of disgust. "What on earth is going on?"

"We wish we knew," Logan replied.

"You've got a missing groom and someone trying to kill the bride," the police officer replied as if the head of Payne Protection had asked him the question. "And my wife thinks my daughter's wedding was a disaster…"

Tanya wasn't going to have a wedding. She opened her mouth to call it off, but then she remembered Stephen and that blood in the groom's quarters. His blood…

What if he was being held for ransom? And she couldn't meet that ransom?

Those thoughts kept running through her head—even as she answered that officer's questions:

No, she hadn't seen anything. She hadn't gotten close enough to the window to look out before the glass shattered. No, she had no idea who might have been behind this attempt or the other one on her life.

She lifted her gaze and caught Cooper staring at her, as if he doubted her. His eyes were narrowed, speculative. Did he have some idea who'd taken Stephen? Who had just tried to kill her?

She waited for him to share his suspicions with the police. But he said nothing to add to the report before they left. He didn't even say anything when his brother told her to pack a bag because *he* was taking her someplace safe.

"But what if someone tries to contact me about Stephen?" she asked.

"Then you'd better be alive to take the call," Logan said. "The purse you left at the church is in my car. Is your cell in there?"

Her face flushed with embarrassment again. "Yes, and the cell is the only phone I have." So she didn't have to worry about a call coming into a landline. She had no reason to stay in her apartment, especially as damaged as it was from the gunfire—the window shattered and drywall dust sprinkling down from the holes in the ceiling, covering the furniture and the hardwood floor.

"Then grab your charger," Logan advised, "and whatever else you need."

"I already have a bag packed." She grabbed a suitcase out of her closet. She'd already had it packed for her honeymoon, which was nothing more exotic than a hotel suite—with separate bedrooms—at an inn on the Lake Michigan shore just outside the city. She had left more lingerie in her drawers than she'd packed, and she was the only one she'd figured would see it. That wasn't going to change just because her groom had.

"I'll take that," Logan offered, reaching for her suitcase.

Cooper finally spoke, asking, "Where are you taking her?"

"Safe house," his brother replied.

He arched a dark brow. "Are you going to tell me where?"

"Doesn't matter," Logan said. "You're not staying there. Parker's taking you to another safe house."

He groaned in protest. "Why can't I just go home?"

"Because Mom gave me orders to make sure both the bride and the groom stay alive to make it to the church tomorrow."

"I don't need Parker to keep me alive," Cooper said, his male pride obviously wounded.

Tanya remembered how hard he had struggled to be his own man growing up—instead of the shadow of his older brothers. She suspected it was why he'd joined the Marines instead of going into the police academy.

Logan snorted. "I know that. I need Parker to keep you away from Tanya."

Her pulse quickened with excitement. Did his brother think that Cooper was attracted to her? Maybe she hadn't been the only one who'd wanted that kiss—that kiss that never happened...

"Mom gave me all kinds of orders based on wedding superstitions," Logan said, "that the bride and groom need to spend the night before the wedding apart or they'll have bad luck."

Tanya laughed now and then flinched at the brittle sound of her own laughter. She probably was on the verge of hysteria brought on by the events of this horrible, horrible day, and by exhaustion. "Bad luck? Mrs. Payne is worried we'll have bad luck?" Another hysterical laugh slipped out. "Like we haven't already? My groom has been...abducted! I've nearly been run down and I've been shot at," she reminded them as if the shattered glass and the holes in her ceiling weren't reminder enough. "What else could go wrong?"

Logan pointed out the obvious. "You or Cooper could get killed."

Her stalker obviously wanted to stop her wedding. So Tanya had no doubt that there would be more attempts on her life and—if the stalker had figured out that Cooper was her new groom—on his, too, before the night was over.

She suspected the night would seem endless, unless it ended—forever.

"You were not supposed to come here," Parker protested as Cooper unlocked the door and stepped inside the condo unit. "This is not the safe house."

Cooper flipped on a switch before stepping inside. "I don't need a safe house."

"Those shots could have been meant for you," Parker pointed out.

He shook his head. "After the car tried running over Tanya? No, the shots were meant for her." Had they been fired high just to scare her? Or had they actually been meant to kill her? His guts clenched with dread and fear. "Are you sure she's safe with Logan?"

Parker laughed. "Have you been gone so long that you've forgotten who Logan is? Logan Payne always keeps his word. If he promised he would keep her safe, he will keep her safe. It's you I'm worried about..."

"Me?" Cooper asked, confused by his brother's concern. "I told you the shots weren't meant for me."

"If someone's figured out you're standing in for the groom, they could have been. Look what happened to Stephen."

"We don't know what happened to Stephen," Cooper reminded him. "That's why we're here." At Stephen's condo.

"I've already been here," Parker said.

The unit was in a high-security high-rise complex. The condo's living room was enormous and its kitchen gourmet with dark cabinets, granite countertops and industrial appliances. Even if she didn't inherit her grandfather's money, Stephen could offer Tanya a much better life than Cooper could. If he could be found…

"But when you were here, you were looking for Stephen."

"And anything that might lead us to him," Parker added. "We didn't find anything."

Cooper picked up a laptop from the coffee table. "Did you look at this?"

Parker shook his head. "It's password protected." He took the computer. "Nikki might be able to crack it, though. But what's she going to find? His kidnapper wouldn't send an email to Stephen. He'd send it to Tanya."

"We don't know that this is a kidnapping." He was beginning to think it less likely with every minute that passed without a ransom call being made.

"We don't know what the hell this is…"

And looking around Stephen's place didn't reveal any more clues. There was no blood here. No signs of a scuffle at all.

There was a suitcase open on Stephen's bed. But he hadn't packed it as Tanya had hers—for their honeymoon. Had he changed his mind? Had he gotten cold feet?

There were no pictures of his fiancée in Stephen's bedroom. The only photo of her anywhere was in the second bedroom that he must have used as an office. It wasn't even the engagement photo of the two of them. It was a photo of the three of them—Stephen, Tanya and him—at their high school graduation, clad in their caps and gowns. He and Stephen had worn maroon and Tanya was in white, standing in the middle of the men, like a candle in the dark.

Had she come between them literally? Maybe it was simple jealousy that had brought on Cooper's doubts…

"Nice picture," Parker said. "I noticed it earlier."

"It's old." And staring at it made Cooper feel old. "Where are the recent photos of them? Of Tanya?"

"Maybe on his phone?" Parker mused. "I take them with mine and never bother printing them off."

Cooper nodded. He did the same when he cared enough about something to take photos, like of his squad. Or some of the Afghani children. Or the countryside that had actually been quite beautiful…

"Nobody found his phone," Cooper recalled.

"It must be with him."

Or with his body.

"Nikki's been trying to track the GPS on it. But she hasn't been able to pick up anything. Maybe the battery's been removed."

"Or the phone destroyed…"

"You don't think he's been kidnapped," Parker said.

He shrugged. "I don't know what to think." Or maybe he was afraid to think it. But a lot of years had passed since that graduation picture. He wasn't the same person he'd been back then. Probably neither was Tanya or Stephen…

"You're not going to find any answers here," Parker said, tucking the laptop under his arm. "We need to get you to that safe house before Logan loses it." His cell phone started to play music. "Speak of the devil…"

Cooper laughed since Parker's ringtone for his twin was "Sympathy for the Devil." He pulled the door closed and followed Parker down the hall to the elevator.

"We'll be there in a little while," he assured his twin.

"We stopped back at Stephen's. No, we didn't really think he'd show up there..." He rolled his eyes at Cooper as the argument continued.

Apparently, the years hadn't changed Logan or Parker, they still fought like the teenage girls Cooper had once accused them of being. He was still grinning over that memory when they stepped off the elevator and crossed the foyer to the outside doors.

A strange sensation chased up and down Cooper's spine and he hesitated before pushing open the doors. But Parker, perhaps distracted with his call, didn't notice Cooper's hesitation, and he continued through them into the dimly lit parking lot.

Cooper had learned long ago to heed his instincts, so he reached for his gun. But before he could draw it from its holster, shots rang out.

Chapter Six

Tanya jerked awake to darkness. But she was not alone. She heard a voice—a deep voice murmuring quietly as the speaker was probably trying not to wake her.

But then the voice rose to a panicked shout. "What the hell's happening? Parker? Cooper?"

She jumped up from the bed and scrambled toward the voice. But she couldn't find the door. She slid her palms along the wall until finally she found the door-knob and turned it.

"What's going on?" she asked as she burst into the hotel suite's sitting room where Logan Payne paced and shouted his brothers' names into his cell phone.

He turned to her in surprise, as if he'd forgotten she had been sleeping in one of the bedrooms of the suite. His eyes were wild with fear and frustration. His brothers needed him, but he had been stuck protecting her. She saw all that on his face—his handsome face that was so like Cooper's.

"What's going on!" she demanded.

He lifted his broad shoulders in a tense shrug. "I don't know." And it was obviously killing him.

"Why are you so worried about them?"

He hesitated, his jaw clenched the way Cooper so

often clenched his, before he finally answered her, "I heard gunshots."

Again. Someone had been shooting at Cooper again. "I thought you sent them to a safe house, too." Apparently that house hadn't been as safe as the one to which Logan had brought her.

"They didn't make it there yet," Logan said. "They stopped at Stephen's condo."

If Stephen had gone back home, he would have called her before now. Even if he had changed his mind about marrying her, he would have called her. Wherever Stephen was, he didn't have access to a phone.

"Why did they go there?" she asked.

"Cooper wanted to search it himself for clues..." Anger flashed in Logan's eyes. "On the job one day and thinks he's a detective..."

"We need to make sure they're all right," she said. And she was grateful now that she'd slept in her clothes instead of changing into something from her suitcase. She actually hadn't meant to, but she'd been too exhausted to change when Logan had brought her to this strange "safe house," which was actually a very small hotel suite in a very obscure hotel.

Logan shook his head. "Not *we*. You're staying here."

"Cooper's getting shot at because of me," she reminded his eldest brother.

"You don't know that."

"He's only been home a couple of days after years of being gone," she said. "There's no reason for anyone else to be shooting at him."

"We don't know that the shots I overheard were being fired at them."

"Stephen's condo isn't exactly in the bad part of town,"

she argued. "It's safe there." Safer than where she lived and definitely more affluent.

"We don't know what happened," Logan said. "So you're going to stay here while I find out."

"You're leaving me alone?" she asked, doubting that either his mother or Cooper would approve of that.

"I know you're afraid," Logan said.

She was afraid. For Cooper and Parker—far more than herself.

"So take me with you," she said, desperate to find out if Cooper was okay. She wasn't about to lose another prospective groom.

"No." Logan shook his head. "You're staying here. And you're staying safe." He lifted his gun from the holster under his arm and held it out to her.

She stared at the weapon and shook her head. "You're going to need that."

"I have another one in the car," he said. "But by the time I get to Stephen's complex, I'm sure the shooting will be all over."

Cooper could be all over. After more than a decade away from his family, he could have been killed days after returning home. Pain clutched her heart at the loss— *the tragic loss*—that would be. And now she wished she had kissed him…if only just to see if it still felt as magical and sensual as she'd remembered all these years.

"So hang on to this," he said as he pressed the gun into her hands.

The metal was cold and heavy and uncomfortable to grasp. She hadn't been deployed like Cooper, but as a social worker she'd seen more than her share of tragedies— many of them caused by guns. She wanted to shove it back onto Logan. But she didn't want to keep him from checking on Cooper and Parker. So she held on to it despite her revulsion.

"And lock yourself in the bedroom," Logan ordered her. "If anyone tries coming through the door without identifying himself, squeeze the trigger and keep shooting until you run out of bullets."

What then?

She would have asked if she hadn't already known the answer. If she used all the bullets and not a single one struck her target, even though she'd tried hard not to break Mrs. Payne's superstitions, she was still out of luck.

"WHAT THE HELL was that?" Parker griped as he lay sprawled across the asphalt of the complex parking lot. "You knocked my phone out of my hand and probably destroyed Stephen's computer."

"You're welcome," Cooper replied.

Parker cursed him as he stretched his arm under a car, grappling for his phone. He cursed again as his fingertips brushed against it and pushed it farther from his reach.

"What's a phone when I just saved your life?"

Parker scoffed, "Sure, you saved my life."

"Someone was firing real bullets at us," Cooper reminded him. And might fire some more if they lifted their heads above the car they crouched behind for cover. "If you think they were blanks, maybe I should have let one hit you."

"You really expect me to thank you?" Parker asked in astonishment.

"That's the usual custom when someone saves another person's life," Cooper said. Maybe he hadn't been gone that long, since he was easily falling back into the old pattern of bantering with his family. "In some countries, that would make you my indentured servant. You would have to wait on me hand and foot in reward for my heroism."

But even as he teased Parker, he listened for more gunshots, for the sound of a car's engine or tires, or a person's footsteps…

"All those damn medals and commendations went straight to your head," Parker griped. "You wouldn't have had to save me if you hadn't put me in danger in the first place."

Cooper sputtered, "How is any of this my fault?"

Parker jammed his shoulder against the rocker panel of the car and stretched his arm farther toward the phone. "You wanted to come here—"

"You came here earlier tonight," he reminded his brother, "and nobody shot at you."

"Yeah, because I'm not getting married tomorrow." He shuddered as if the mere thought of marriage horrified him, and inadvertently pushed the phone farther to the other side of the car.

If they were certain that the shooter was gone, they could have gotten up and walked around to the other side. But maybe that was what the assailant was waiting for…a clear shot.

Cooper had knocked Parker down so quickly and dropped to the ground himself that the shooter had only managed a couple of shots.

Had no one else heard them? No sirens wailed—not even in the distance. Parker needed that phone to call 911 since Cooper had left his in the car with the battery pulled out of it so that nobody could track it. Their car was parked on the other side of the lot.

Struggling to keep his face straight as he uttered the lie, he said, "I thought those shots were meant for you."

"Me?" Parker was all astonished sounding again.

"You're the playboy." He had been in high school, and according to the letters he received from Nikki while he was overseas, that hadn't changed. "You must have pissed off a husband or boyfriend lately."

Parker shuddered again as if in remembrance. "Not lately." He hesitated as if considering. "No, not lately." He nudged Cooper's shoulder. "Those shots were meant for you, little brother. You're the one marrying the Grim Reaper bride."

"Hey!" He smacked his brother upside the head, like Logan so often had his twin and Cooper. "Don't call her that!"

Parker smacked him back. "I know she's hot and you've always had this crush on her, but you need to remember that you're not marrying her for real. And if that shooter has his way, you're not going to marry her at all."

They paused in their scuffle to listen. Had a door opened and shut? Was someone here?

"I was supposed to take you right to that safe house," Parker said in a low grumble. "If that shooter doesn't kill us, Logan will…"

Something scraped against the asphalt, and Cooper peered under the car to see a pair of dark shoes advancing toward them. The man stopped on the other side of the car, then leaned down and picked up Parker's phone.

"Hey, Paula, Cathy—quit your bickering and stop cowering behind that car," Logan said with a chuckle of amusement and relief.

"We are not cowering," Cooper informed his eldest brother. But his pride stung over how Logan had found them arguing behind a vehicle. He must have secured the scene first, though, so Cooper jumped up from the pavement. "We took cover."

"While I was on the phone with Parker, I heard the shots," Logan said. "I take it you're both okay." He narrowed his eyes and studied Cooper then glanced down at his twin. "Neither of you got hit?"

Parker stood up and rubbed his ear. "I wouldn't say that. I took quite a hit from our little brother."

"Where's Tanya?" Cooper asked. He didn't have time for their teasing. He peered around the parking lot, looking for Logan's vehicle. "You didn't bring her along, did you?"

Logan shook his head. "She's at the safe house."

His pulse quickening with anxiety, he asked, "Alone? Did you leave her alone?"

"There's another guard on perimeter duty."

"Someone sitting in a car out front?" he asked. "Like he couldn't be compromised…" His stomach lurched as a horrible realization dawned on him. "What if these shots were a diversion? A way to lure you away from her?"

Logan shook his head. "Like the shooter would know I would be on the phone with Parker. Hell, he probably doesn't even know Tanya was with me."

"He could have been watching back at her place." From the threats Cooper had found packed away in that box, it looked like this person had been stalking her for years. "He could have seen who she left with and followed you."

Logan's pride was obviously stung now. He lifted his chin. "I was *not* followed."

"Even you can't be sure of that," Cooper challenged him.

Just the tiniest flicker of doubt flashed in Logan's eyes. "Damn it. Damn you…"

"Tell me where she is!" he demanded. The first light of dawn streaked across the dark sky. It was now his wedding day. His mother's superstitions be damned, he had to check on his bride—to make sure that he hadn't already lost her.

THE HOTEL SUITE had been eerily silent for so long that Tanya had become aware of noises she had never heard before—like the sound of her own blood rushing through her veins. The soft thump of her racing pulse. The whispery *whoosh* of her breaths coming in and out of her nose.

How long had Logan been gone? Too long for Parker and Cooper to be all right. If they hadn't been hurt, he would have come back by now.

Unless the shots had been a trap to lure Logan away from her...

She had known there would be another attempt on her life—another attempt to stop her from marrying and inheriting. She should have known that no place would be safe enough for her.

Or Cooper...

She never should have agreed with his becoming her groom. But she'd worried that she might need that money to pay a ransom for Stephen's safe return. But there had been no call, no demand. She glanced at her phone and noticed that the screen had gone dark. Was it just in sleep mode?

She tapped the screen, but it remained black. She had plugged the phone into the charger, but maybe the charger wasn't plugged into a live outlet. Was it one of those that was connected to the wall switch?

What if she'd missed the ransom call because her phone was dead?

She wanted to flip on the switch by the door, but then the lights would come on, too. And she preferred sitting in the dark. That way, if someone got inside the suite, they might not check her room since there would be no light streaking beneath the door. They might think that she had left with Logan.

She should have left with Logan. Then she wouldn't be helplessly waiting for news about Cooper. She couldn't lose Stephen and him in one night.

Her heart was beating harder now, so loudly that it deafened her to the other noises she should have heard. The noises, like the door to the hall opening, like the footsteps that might have warned her that she was no longer alone in the safe house.

But she had no clue she wasn't alone anymore until the doorknob rattled. She'd locked it, but the lock was flimsy. Heck, so was the door. It wouldn't take much for someone to force his way inside. Or shoot his way inside...

But she had a gun now, too. She clasped it in hands that had gone clammy and numb from holding the heavy weapon. Could she uncurl her fingers enough to pull the trigger?

Could she pull the trigger at all? And fire bullets into another human being?

Suddenly, the door opened. And she squeezed...

Chapter Seven

"Damn it," was the least offensive of Cooper's curses as he ducked. The bullet tunneled into the woodwork near his shoulder.

And Tanya screamed and dropped the gun.

Instead of ducking again, Cooper launched himself at her—knocking her back onto the bed in case the gun fired another round when it hit the ground. But it only spun across the threadbare carpet like a bottle at a game of spin the bottle. It stopped with the barrel pointing at them.

Cooper cursed again because he was tempted to kiss her—especially when she cupped his face in her hands and stared up at him as if she wanted his kiss, too.

"You're alive," she murmured.

"No thanks to you," he reminded them both. "I guess Logan was right when he said I needed protecting from you." He'd known she was lying when she said she wouldn't hurt him. He'd had no doubt she would hurt him—just as she had when they were kids and she'd so readily agreed with him that they were just friends. "I didn't think *you* would shoot me, though."

Tears sprang to her eyes, brightening the already vivid green. Her hands dropped from his face to the bed where she grasped the sheets. "I'm sorry! I'm so sorry! I thought you were someone else…"

"My brother? I was tempted to shoot him myself when I realized he'd left you alone." Since the guard Logan had stationed outside had fallen asleep in a car parked in the lot, he had essentially left her all alone.

"I shouldn't have fired the gun until I saw who it was," she said. "But your brother told me to shoot anyone who came through the door without announcing himself."

"And announcing myself in Afghanistan would have gotten me killed for sure," Cooper mused. "But I'm beginning to think I was safer there—I actually may have gotten shot at less."

She shuddered. "Logan was right? He heard shots on the phone?"

Cooper nodded.

"Outside Stephen's condo?"

Cooper nodded again. "Just as we were leaving the complex, someone started shooting. Neither of us got hit. They may have only been firing to scare us."

"To scare *you,*" she said, "so you won't marry me."

"Don't worry," he assured her. "I don't scare easily."

"That's not good," she said. "Because if he can't scare you off, he'll try to kill you."

The way *he* had her.

"That's why I have to call off the wedding—to keep you alive," she said.

"What about a ransom demand on Stephen? You won't be able to meet it if you don't marry."

Her hips arching into his, she wriggled beneath him until she slid out from under him. Then she grabbed up the phone and charger and plugged it into another outlet. "No missed calls," she said with a sigh of relief. Then her brow furrowed. "No ransom call…"

"We don't know that there won't be one," Cooper pointed out.

"Wouldn't it have been made already?" she asked anxiously. "Why would they wait?"

He shrugged. "To see if you actually can get the money together."

"But if they don't want money to give Stephen back, we'll have gotten married for nothing."

His pride stung—at least that was all he hoped it was—that she obviously did not want to marry him. But then, Cooper hadn't wanted to marry her either. "We can fix that then."

"An annulment," she said with a sigh of relief. "I was going to tell you that you don't have to worry that I'll think this is permanent. As soon as I get my inheritance, we'll get divorced. But an annulment is better..."

Because with an annulment, it would be as if they had never been married. But the only way an annulment could be granted quickly was if the marriage was never consummated. He ignored the flash of disappointment he felt; he'd known this wasn't going to be a real marriage.

He wasn't the real groom. Stephen was. Cooper was just the stand-in groom. Stephen was the man she loved; she'd told him herself. Cooper was...just the man she'd nearly shot.

"Fine," he agreed just as readily as she had agreed that they were just friends all those years ago. "We'll get an annulment. But first we have to get married."

She shivered as if the prospect terrified her. "I don't want to put you in danger, though."

And he realized she was terrified for *him*. He reached out for her hand and then tugged her back down onto the bed next to him. "You're not putting me in danger."

She shook her head. "By marrying you, I am."

"You're not the one trying to shoot me," he said. "Well, at least not until just now."

"I'm really, really sorry," she apologized again, her beautiful face tense with regret and fear. "I never should have taken the gun from your brother."

Anger surged through Cooper again. "He never should have left you alone."

Logan was the boss, but Cooper wouldn't let bad decisions like that go unchallenged—professionally or personally.

"He was worried about you and Parker when he heard the shots," she defended. "I was worried, too." She entwined her fingers with his. "I don't want anything to happen to you."

She probably only said that because of their past friendship—because they had once been so close. But they hadn't been for years. She'd written letters after he left, but he hadn't replied to hers. He hadn't wanted to think about her moving on with her life when he had just moved.

"I survived three deployments," he reminded her. "I'll be fine." And he intended to make sure that she would be, too.

She lifted her other hand to his face and skimmed her fingers along his jaw. Her fingers trembled. "I don't want anything to happen to you…"

His heart lurched. Could she actually care about him?

"Your family worried so much when you were gone," she said. "If something happened to you now…"

"It won't." Because he wasn't going to risk his heart on her again. She was more concerned about his family than she was him.

She nodded. "Okay, then, if you're certain you'll be safe, I'll marry you."

He wouldn't be safe—not even with his resolve to not risk his heart on her. She was so damn beautiful that he doubted he would be able to control his attraction to her. Even now he was so tempted to lean forward, to close the distance between them and press his lips to hers.

But then she was the one arching up and forward and closing the distance between them. "Thank you," she murmured.

Maybe she meant to kiss his cheek.

She probably meant to kiss his cheek.

But Cooper turned his head, and her mouth met his. It should have been just a quick peck then. But she gasped and the kiss deepened. Cooper couldn't help himself—he dipped his tongue between her parted lips and tasted her.

She was even sweeter than he remembered.

Her fingers clasped his face and she kissed him back, her tongue flicking across his. Touching. Teasing...

They weren't teenagers anymore. A kiss wasn't just a kiss. They knew where it could lead, and they were sitting on a bed. Cooper fought for control and pulled back, just as Tanya did the same.

Her face flushed and eyes widened, she panted for breath. She moved her lips, but no words formed. Obviously she didn't have any idea what to say either.

Cooper glanced down to where the gun barrel pointed at them like that spin-the-bottle. But that wasn't why she'd kissed him. She had obviously only meant to kiss his cheek—probably out of gratitude.

But Cooper was less concerned about why she'd kissed him than he was about why he'd kissed her. He knew she loved another man—a man who had always been a good friend to him, even when Cooper had physically and emotionally let distance grow between them. Kissing the man's fiancée was an act of betrayal.

Unless…

No, he had no proof. Not yet. He had no reason for his suspicions. Except maybe he wanted to think the worst so that he wouldn't feel so damn guilty.

Shaking his head, he murmured, "That didn't happen."

Her eyes still wide, she nodded in agreement.

"I wasn't even here," he said.

"What?"

"If my mother asks, you didn't see me last night or this morning…"

Her lips curved into a slight smile. "Her wedding traditions?"

"Superstitions," he corrected her. "We are not to see each other until…"

Light streaked through the blinds at the hotel room window. It was his wedding day.

"Until we meet again at the church," she finished for him.

"Try to get some sleep," he suggested.

"What about you?"

He shrugged. After that kiss? He doubted he would be able to close his eyes without imagining where that kiss could have led, without anticipating a honeymoon that would never happen, thanks to her wanting an annulment. "I don't need much sleep anymore."

"Even after today?" she asked, her thick lashes blinking as she struggled against exhaustion to keep her eyes open.

He'd had longer, more dangerous days. He gently pushed her back until she lay down on the bed. Then he pulled the blanket over her, as exhaustion overwhelmed her and she fell asleep. He needed to stand up, needed to step away from the bed before he was tempted to crawl into it with her and hold her. But he couldn't stop staring at her beautiful face. It had been so long since he'd seen her. And tonight he'd nearly lost her—twice.

But then he sighed as he remembered that she wasn't his to lose. A shadow fell across the floor, and he reached for his weapon.

"I thought you didn't want to come to their wedding because you didn't care anymore," Logan remarked from the doorway. "But that's not the case at all. You didn't want to come because you care too much."

He pulled his hand away from his holster and replied to his brother, "She and Stephen were my best friends in high school. They helped me through losing Dad."

"She's more than a friend to you."

He shook his head in denial, but still he couldn't stop staring at her. "No."

"Maybe I'm wrong," Logan said, but his tone indicated he thought otherwise. "But she was right. You should get some sleep."

"I need to make sure she stays safe."

"I'll do that," Logan said.

When Cooper turned toward him, his older brother lifted his hands as if to ward off an attack. "I won't leave her again even if you're begging me for help."

"I won't…" If he wound up begging, it wouldn't be for Logan.

"Take my help tonight," Logan said, "because you're going to be primary protection for her at the wedding and after…"

On that honeymoon. But they wouldn't get to that if they didn't survive the wedding. Someone was so determined to stop that, judging from the recent shooting attempts, he or she didn't seem to care who died—the bride or the groom.

HOURS HAD PASSED, but Tanya's lips still tingled from that kiss. What had she been thinking to kiss Cooper Payne?

He wasn't the teenage boy with whom she had once been friends. He was a man now, and his kiss had proven that. But then, even as a boy, he'd kissed like a man.

She released a shaky breath.

"It's going to be okay," Mrs. Payne promised as she opened the bride's dressing room door and ushered Tanya inside. Sunshine bathed the room, setting its soft pink walls and white wainscoting aglow.

And Tanya nearly believed her. She had always had so much admiration for Mrs. Payne. Tanya's mother had wallowed in self-pity after her husband chose money over a life with her and her daughters. But Cooper's mother had lost the love of her life through a horrible tragedy and yet she had put aside her own anguish and heartbreak to be the rock her children had needed her to be.

Tanya had leaned on her all those years ago herself. And she leaned on her now, giving her a big hug. "Thank you for everything you've done."

Mrs. Payne patted her back. "You're like one of my own, sweetheart. I would do anything for you."

That was the kind of mother Tanya hoped to be some-day. But when would that day be? She had to live through this wedding and subsequent annulment to have hope of ever having another wedding—a real one.

"I'm so sorry that I'm putting your family in danger," Tanya continued. The Paynes had already been through too much tragedy. She hoped she wouldn't bring another one upon them.

"You are not responsible for any of this, Tanya." Mrs. Payne chuckled. "And, honey, my boys have been put-ting themselves in danger since the day they were each born. Climbing trees too high. Riding bikes too fast. Then joining the police force and the Marines." She shook her head and sighed.

When Cooper had joined the service after high school, Tanya had been almost relieved that they had never taken their relationship beyond friendship. She would have been so worried about him, so devastated if anything happened to him...

"Isn't that hard on you?" Tanya asked. "After what happened..."

"To their father?" Mrs. Payne uttered another sigh, a wistful one, and her face softened—the faint lines she had entirely disappearing so that she looked like the young girl she must have been when she fell in love with Mr. Payne. "Having them act so much like their father has kept him alive for me—and probably for them."

"But they put their lives at risk..."

Mrs. Payne let out an indelicate snort. "Living puts our lives at risk—driving a car, taking a bus, going to the mall or a movie...bad things happen everywhere. Not just Afghanistan. Cooper survived that—he can survive anything."

Tanya wasn't as confident of that as his mother.

The older woman gave her a slight nudge toward the garment bag hanging from the hook on the wall. "Start getting dressed, honey. Your sister and Nikki are on their way."

"Rochelle?" She tensed with shock and concern. "She's still going to stand up there with me?"

"She's your sister. Family sticks together."

The Payne family definitely did, but not the Chesterfield family. Money had always divided them and probably always would.

Knuckles wrapped against the door. "That better not

be Cooper. I told him to stay away from you until the wedding." She opened the door to Tanya's grandfather's lawyer.

"I'm sorry to interrupt," Mr. Gregory said. "But I really need a word with Ms. Chesterfield."

"Tanya," she corrected him as she so often had had to over the years. Her grandfather may have demanded formality but it made her uncomfortable.

Mrs. Payne studied the handsome gray-haired man intently before nodding. "You'll do…"

The lawyer's face reddened and he uttered, "Excuse me, ma'am?"

Mrs. Payne had been single a long time. Perhaps she was finally ready to envision a future for herself instead of just helping brides and grooms get ready for theirs.

"Tanya needs someone to walk her down the aisle," Mrs. Payne explained. "I was going to enlist my eldest boy, but it would be better to have someone who's been part of Tanya's life."

Arthur Gregory had been a part of her life for a long time—since before his hair had gone gray and he'd developed lines around his dark eyes and his tightly lipped mouth.

"I'm sure Ms. Chesterfield would rather—"

"No," Tanya interrupted him. "I would be happy to have you walk me down…" To her stand-in groom. If not for Stephen's disappearance, Cooper probably wouldn't have even attended the wedding.

"I'll leave you two to discuss it," Mrs. Payne said as she bustled from the room and closed the door behind herself.

The lawyer stared after the petite woman. "She's something else…"

If Tanya remembered correctly, Mr. Gregory had never married. "Mrs. Payne is wonderful."

"But misguided," the lawyer said.

"I'm sorry she enlisted you in the wedding," Tanya apologized. "If it makes you uncomfortable, you don't have to participate."

"The whole wedding makes me uncomfortable," he admitted.

She had a million reasons of her own, but she asked, "Why?"

"I'm worried that these people may be taking advantage of you."

If anything, it was the reverse, she was taking advantage of them. "They are helping me."

"But you wouldn't need help if Stephen hadn't disappeared," he said.

"Exactly."

"He disappeared from *here*." The lawyer stared at her as if that meant something.

She arched a brow in question.

"And immediately after that, *she* suggested that her son take his place."

Tanya wasn't exactly certain why Mrs. Payne had pushed Cooper into that—unless she wanted them together. Had she been aware all those years ago that Tanya had had a crush on her son?

"That was very sweet of her to help me out. I only have a couple of days until I turn thirty." And Stephen hadn't been found yet. She didn't dare wait until the last day—in case that ransom demand was made.

"It was perhaps too convenient," Mr. Gregory suggested.

"What are you saying?"

"Your grandfather always worried that you and your sister would be taken advantage of because of your inheritance."

Like their father had taken advantage of their mother. What little money her father had left her, their mother had used to track down their father. She'd obviously intended to use it to buy back the man's love that her father had bought off. Tanya and Rochelle hadn't seen or heard from her since she'd left.

Her voice sharp in defense of her friends, she replied, "That is not the case with the Paynes."

"Your grandfather did not trust Cooper Payne," Mr. Gregory said. "He warned the boy years ago—"

"He what?" she gasped, both shocked and horrified. "Did he try to buy off Cooper, too?"

The lawyer shook his head. "He just pointed out to him that you were out of his league."

She would like to believe that her grandfather wouldn't have done such a humiliating thing to her and Cooper, but she knew better. The old man had enjoyed humiliating and manipulating people, especially his own family.

"You *still* are out of his league, Tanya," Mr. Gregory continued. "The only reason you're marrying him is because your real groom conveniently disappeared."

Remembering all that spattered blood, she flinched. "There was nothing convenient about Stephen's disappearance." Terrifying? Yes. Convenient? No.

"It is convenient for Cooper Payne since he's stepping in as your groom. I can't believe that his mother managed to obtain a marriage license at such short notice."

Neither could Tanya, but Mrs. Payne was definitely a full-service wedding planner. There was nothing she wouldn't do for a bride.

It wasn't awe in the lawyer's voice, though. It was suspicion. Tanya narrowed her eyes and glared at Mr. Gregory. "If you're implying that the Paynes are responsible for what happened to Stephen, you're dead wrong."

"This is why your grandfather put the stipulation on your inheritance," the lawyer said cynically, "because you tend to be too naive and trusting."

She laughed. No one had *ever* accused her of being either of those things. "Grandfather didn't know me." Because he'd never made the effort. "And neither do you. Moreover, you don't know the Paynes at all. They are known for their honor and protectiveness. They would never harm anyone."

"You think that is still true of Cooper?" he asked her. "He's been to war. You don't know how that can change a man. He isn't the boy you remember."

Tanya had thought so, too, but then she had seen glimpses of that boy—in his camaraderie with his family and his concern for her and Stephen. And in his kiss...

"Why would Cooper hurt Stephen?" she asked.

"Jealousy," he suggested. "Over you..."

"We were never anything but friends." Because that was the way he'd wanted to keep it.

Mr. Gregory chuckled. "The kid mooned around after you. He had a major crush on you. That was why your grandfather told him to stay away from you."

She'd thought he'd stopped coming to her house because he'd considered it a mausoleum. She hadn't minded. She and Stephen had both liked it at his house better. The Payne household was warm and noisy and full of love.

"That was a long time ago," Tanya reminded him.

The lawyer shrugged. "So maybe it's about money now. He's probably not making much working for his family. But marrying you..."

"You think Cooper is marrying me for my money?" She nearly laughed again since it was really the reverse. *She* was marrying *him* for her money. "That's ridiculous."

She'd overheard his argument with his family. The last thing he'd wanted to do was marry her.

"Then have him sign a prenup," he suggested, and he patted his ever-present dark leather briefcase, "and prove that he has no interest in your inheritance."

She shook her head. "I can't ask him to do that..." Not when he was already making a sacrifice for her. Or, actually, for Stephen. He had only agreed to marry her in case someone demanded a ransom for his return.

He hadn't been missing a whole day yet. There was time. Time to bring him back safely from wherever he'd been taken.

"If you can't ask him, I will," Mr. Gregory offered as he turned for the door.

Tanya grabbed his briefcase to stop him. "No!"

The last thing she needed was her grandfather's lawyer insulting Cooper as her grandfather must have all those years ago. Was that why he'd said they should just be friends? What would he have done if she'd disagreed with him?

Too many years had passed. The past was the past. She had to accept that she would never know now.

"You don't trust him either," the lawyer remarked. "You think he's only marrying you for the money. Tanya, it's not too late. You need to stop this wedding."

She shook her head.

"Take a little time," he urged her. "Think about it. You'll realize you can't marry a man that you can't trust."

It wasn't Cooper that she wasn't trusting at the moment. She opened the door for the lawyer to show him out. "I'd prefer to have Logan Payne walk me down the aisle," she said, dismissing him.

"I wouldn't walk you down the aisle to Cooper Payne anyway," he told her. "Your grandfather would haunt me for certain."

Maybe that was who was causing Tanya all her grief—her grandfather's ghost. She wouldn't put it past the old man to haunt her, especially if he had any idea what she'd intended to do with her inheritance.

But first she had to marry to inherit. She drew in a deep breath to brace herself before reaching for the zipper on the garment bag. As she pulled down the tab, bits of lace and satin fell onto the floor like those black petals from the dead roses.

Someone had hacked the heavy material into small pieces. How much hate did it take for someone to be so vindictive? So malicious?

Tears stung her eyes and she shuddered in dread.

The doorknob rattled. Maybe whoever had cut up her dress had returned to do the same to her.

Chapter Eight

His exit blocked, Cooper was trapped inside the blood-spattered groom's quarters. The police had only just released the crime scene that morning. Cooper hoped they'd found something when they'd processed the room that would lead to whoever had taken Stephen. He wanted his friend safe and unharmed. But Stephen wasn't his only concern...

"Get the hell out of my way," he threatened, "or I'll show you what I learned in the Marines—all the ways I learned how to hurt someone."

"You wouldn't hurt me," Parker said, but a tiny flicker of doubt passed through his bright blue eyes. "I kept you safe last night."

"I saved your life," Cooper reminded him.

Parker shook his head. "I was talking about later." A furrow formed in his brow. "Or was it earlier this morning? I stood watch so you could get some sleep."

"You stood watch? On your back?" Cooper chuckled. "You kept me awake with your snoring."

"It wasn't my snoring that kept you awake," Parker said.

And he was right. It hadn't been concern for Tanya's safety either—he'd trusted that Logan wouldn't leave her again, that he would definitely make sure she arrived safely at the church. It had been concern for his own sanity—after that kiss—that had kept Cooper from getting any sleep.

"Wedding jitters kept you awake," Parker said. He tugged at his bow tie as his neck reddened. "I don't blame you. This damn thing feels like a noose."

"It's going to feel more like one if you don't let me pass you," Cooper threatened.

Parker chuckled. "I understand wanting to make a break for it, but I promised Mom that I wouldn't just get you to the church but I'd get you to the altar, too."

"I have to go to the bride's room," Cooper said.

Parker shook his head. "You're not backing out now."

"Don't worry," Cooper said. "It's too late for Mom to get your name on the marriage license instead of mine."

"It's too late for you to back out, too," Parker said, "because if this is about the ransom and she doesn't get the money…"

Stephen would be killed. "Has anyone called with a ransom demand?" The last he'd heard nobody had yet, but that had been hours ago…in Tanya's hotel room right before they'd kissed.

"According to Logan," his twin relayed, "no."

"This isn't about ransom," Cooper said, "but it is about the money."

"You think you've figured it out," Parker realized.

He shrugged since he had no proof. His biggest concern was that his suspicions were correct. And that the bride was alone with the person who wanted her dead.

Instead of reasoning with Parker, he just shoved him aside and hurried out into the empty church. No guests had arrived yet. Hell, it was his wedding, and he wasn't even sure who had been invited. Only the wedding party had arrived. Him as the groom and Parker as his best man.

According to Logan, the bride had arrived safely, too. But had she stayed that way?

He rushed down the aisle to the vestibule and knocked on the door next to the restrooms. No one responded, so he pounded harder. "Open up!"

The lock clicked and the door creaked open only a couple of inches. A chocolate-brown eye narrowed and glared at him. "What are you doing here?"

He lifted a brow and then made a show of glancing down at his tux. "I don't know. What am I doing here—in a monkey suit?"

"You're a monkey?" his sister teased.

His heart lurched at her laughter. God, he'd missed his family. He'd missed his siblings' relentless teasing and his mother's relentless bossing. He had missed someone else, too.

Her voice called out to his sister. "Nikki, is that Cooper? Has he changed his mind?"

"He has if he's as smart as you've always said he was," a bitter voice chimed in. Despite her hysterical outburst the night before, Rochelle had showed up to support her sister. Or sabotage her?

"You can't see her," Nikki told him. "Mom would have a fit over the bad luck you'd have if the groom saw the bride before the wedding."

Mom and her damn superstitions...

He assured her, "I don't want to see the bride." Again. He'd already seen her on the morning of their wedding day; he had already kissed the bride.

"Well, if you're here about that other thing—" she lowered her voice so only he could hear her "—Stephen's computer..."

"Have you made any progress?"

"I might have if it hadn't gotten smashed up..."

He flinched with regret. He needed to know what was on that computer. "Is it beyond repair?"

"No," she assured him. "It's just going to take me a little while longer. And we're kind of busy at the moment." She lowered her voice again. "Someone cut up Tanya's wedding dress."

His heart clenched. "Is she all right?"

"Yeah, Mom fixed it."

"The dress?"

"No, there was no fixing that dress," she said with a shudder. "It was completely destroyed."

And his suspicions increased. Cutting up a dress was an act of incredible jealousy and pettiness.

"Mom found her another dress." Nikki uttered a wistful sigh. "Wait until you see her…"

He stepped forward, but his sister shoved on his chest and pushed him back. "You're going to have to wait," she told him. "Mom's gone above and beyond for this wedding and you're not going to ruin it. You are not seeing the bride."

"I actually want to see the maid of honor."

Nikki opened the door a little farther. She wore a dress in some bronze color that complemented her reddish hair. She narrowed her brown eyes and glared at him. "I know what you're thinking, and you're wrong."

He nodded and acknowledged, "I might be. Let me talk to her."

Rochelle pushed past her friend and stepped into the vestibule with Cooper. She wore the same bronze dress as his sister but it wasn't nearly as flattering. Maybe that was because of the resentful look on her face. She hadn't bothered doing anything with her hair either; it hung in lank strings around her bare shoulders. "Have you come to your senses yet?" she asked.

"Maybe…" he murmured as he studied her face. Her eyes, a grayer shade of green than Tanya's, were red-rimmed and swollen as if she'd cried all night. That could just be what she did every time she got drunk. He had met his share of sloppy drunks over the years. Or maybe she had been that upset over Stephen's disappearance.

How upset had she been over his engagement to her sister?

She expelled a shaky breath of relief. "That's good. You shouldn't marry my sister."

"Why not?" he asked. "Do you want your grandfather's inheritance all to yourself?"

She sucked in a breath. "I—I don't care about his money."

"What do you care about?" he asked. "Stephen?"

Tears shimmered in her eyes and she nodded again. "She didn't care about him at all."

"Then why would she marry him?"

"For the money, that's all she cares about," Rochelle said. "No, that's not true."

"No," he agreed. Tanya had become a social worker, she wouldn't have done that if she didn't care about other people. And she wouldn't have been promoted to supervisor if she didn't care enough about her job to be good at it.

"You," Rochelle said, her resentment now turning on him. "She always had a crush on you."

He would have told her how wrong she was, that Tanya had only wanted to be his friend, but he didn't want to interrupt Rochelle. The more upset she got, the more she might reveal.

"So your marrying her is exactly what she wants," she said, bitterness making her voice sharp and her face ugly. "And Tanya always gets what she wants."

And Cooper suspected that Rochelle always wanted what Tanya had.

"Have you talked to Stephen?" he asked.

She gasped. "Of course not."

"Why 'of course not'?"

"He's missing."

"Yes," he said. "Do you know where he is?"

She gasped again. "You think I have something to do with his disappearance?"

"I think you're jealous that he was going to marry your sister," he said, and he had no doubt that he was right about that. He just wasn't sure about the rest of his suspicions. "And jealous women can be quite dangerous…"

She stepped closer to him, her eyes bright and her nostrils flaring. "You have no idea how dangerous I can be."

He was afraid that he might have a pretty accurate idea.

She stepped back and shook her head. "You know, marry my sister with my blessing. I think the two of you deserve each other." She stepped back inside the bride's room and slammed the door behind her.

"You don't have Parker's way with the ladies," Logan remarked as he joined Cooper in the vestibule.

"Neither do you." Which was more ironic since they looked almost exactly alike. Logan wore his hair shorter than Parker's but not as short as Cooper's military cut.

"That's fine with me," Logan remarked. "I would rather stay single than do what you're about to do." He pointed toward the church. "Parker and the reverend are waiting for you."

"Did Mom send you to get me?"

He shook his head. "No, to get Tanya."

"Déjà vu."

"I'm walking her down the aisle."

She had no one else to do it. Her father had abandoned his family. Her original groom had disappeared. That left only Cooper and his family. He hoped they would be enough to keep her safe.

His mom stepped out of the church and crooked her finger, beckoning him inside. Unlike his siblings, he didn't always blindly obey his mother. She hadn't wanted him to enlist but he had. He had even fought her plan the night before…until he had realized that she was right.

The best way to keep Tanya safe was to marry her. But who was going to keep *him* safe? Because the minute he saw her looking both ethereal and sexy in white lace, he realized that he was in the most danger in which he had ever been. He was in danger of falling irrevocably in love with the woman about to become his wife.

IN HIS BLACK TUXEDO and white pleated shirt, Cooper Payne looked so handsome that he completely stole Tanya's breath. He wouldn't have fit in Stephen's tuxedo. Mrs. Payne must have extra suits available the way she had dresses.

Actually, she'd had only one extra dress on hand. A very special dress…

Cooper's gaze met hers and his eyes widened. Was that because he recognized his mother's dress?

Tanya had the moment Mrs. Payne had brought it to her to replace the destroyed dress. She had seen that dress in the wedding portrait that hung over the mantel in the Payne living room. And she had refused to wear it. The woman that Cooper was going to marry for real—*for a happily-ever-after not just until we get an annulment*—deserved to wear that dress.

Not Tanya.

But Mrs. Payne had insisted in that gracious, indomitable manner of hers that tolerated no refusal or argument. And as she'd also pointed out, Tanya had no other options. Unless she wanted to get married in jeans and a sweater, she had to wear Mrs. Payne's wedding dress.

Maybe she should have gone with the jeans—then she wouldn't feel like such a fraud. Actually, she felt like a bride. A real one. Especially with how intently her groom was staring at her.

The strapless gown was all vintage lace and sparkling beads with a formfitting silhouette. Much more formfitting on Tanya than it had been on the petite bride who'd originally worn it. Mrs. Payne must have worn high heels so that the hem hadn't dragged on the floor. Tanya had forgone shoes. She felt the runner under her bare feet, the red velvet soft against her skin. Each step brought her closer to the altar.

To her groom.

As it had the night before, her heart pounded so loudly that she heard it as well as her blood rushing in her ears. The organ was drowned out. She never heard what Logan said to her as he leaned down and kissed her cheek. Even the first words the minister spoke were lost to her.

Then Cooper took her hands in both of his and her heart stopped beating entirely for a moment. She felt like that teenage girl she'd once been—the one who'd dreamed every night of Cooper Payne declaring his love for her. But then she reminded herself that all that Cooper had ever declared for her was friendship.

She would like to believe that he'd only done that because her grandfather had warned him off. But if Cooper really wanted something, like joining the Marines, he hadn't let anyone scare him off or talk him out of it. Just as he hadn't let getting shot at—twice—the night before scare him away from marrying her. But he wasn't marrying her for her.

He hadn't really wanted her. Then. Or now.

He was marrying her for Stephen—for his safe return. If Stephen was safe...

Was it already too late to save him?

Tears burned her eyes, blurring her vision even more than the veil that Mrs. Payne had also loaned her. It was a thin, delicate lace through which Tanya had had no problem seeing earlier.

"Do you take this man to be your husband, Tanya?" the minister prodded her as if he'd asked the question before.

A couple coughs disrupted the eerie silence of the church. But there weren't many guests. Even when she was going to marry Stephen, she had insisted on keeping the guest list to a minimum. And now Stephen's family and friends weren't present—thanks to the calls Mrs. Payne had made.

It would have been more than just awkward to marry another man in front of them. They wouldn't have understood that she was doing this for him—for Stephen.

Cooper squeezed her hands and nodded as if in encouragement.

And Tanya found herself opening her mouth and whispering the words, "I do."

But was she doing this for Stephen or for herself? Because she was fulfilling that childhood fantasy she'd had of one day marrying Cooper Payne. But in her fantasy, Cooper loved her and wanted to become her husband.

And as he'd had to with her, the minister had to repeat his question to Cooper, "Do you take this woman to be your wife?"

She stared up into Cooper's vivid blue eyes. Like the

minister and those few guests, most of which were his family, she waited for his reply. She wouldn't blame him if he changed his mind—if he refused to marry her.

She held her breath. And the church grew eerily quiet again.

Cooper cleared his throat and finally spoke, "I do."

For a moment Tanya let herself believe it was real—that Cooper Payne was so in love with her that he wanted to become her husband. That he wanted a happily-ever-after with her—and not just until the annulment.

Tears of happiness burned her eyes and she furiously blinked as she tried to clear her vision. But the tears kept burning her eyes and the back of her throat.

She coughed and choked, struggling to breathe. Finally she realized that it wasn't tears of emotion but smoke that was blurring her vision.

The church was on fire.

Tanya knew it couldn't be an accident, not after everything that had happened last night. It was arson. Someone had purposely set the church on fire. The only question was, had the exits been blocked or would they be able to escape the building before flames engulfed the guests and the groom?

She would be dead long before the flames claimed her. Tanya's lungs burned and her airway swelled as she struggled for breath. The asthma that had haunted her childhood flared again, choking her. Usually her asthma only acted up in the spring with seasonal allergies or in the winter if she was unfortunate enough to catch a cold.

But smoke had always been her biggest trigger. Cigarette smoke and bonfires had brought on embarrassing and life-threatening attacks during her teenage years. Back then, her inhaler had saved her. But she didn't have it with her now. It was in her purse, which she had left in the bride's dressing room.

She would never make it that far before passing out—before dying. Mrs. Payne had definitely been right to be superstitious. Seeing the groom before her wedding had brought Tanya terrible, fatal luck…

Chapter Nine

Cooper caught the man's arm, holding him in place before he could run as the others had toward the vestibule. "Do it!" he ordered the minister. "Pronounce us man and wife!"

The man choked and sputtered, the words whispered and hoarse, "I now pronounce you man and wife."

It was official. Tanya Chesterfield was not just his bride—she was now his wife. But she was coughing harder than the others, her shoulders shaking and body trembling as she struggled for breath.

Would he soon become her widower?

He caught her up in his arms and followed the others toward those doors at the back of the church. Logan carried their mother. With an arm around each of them, Parker helped both Rochelle and Nikki while the lawyer and the minister hurried out ahead of Cooper and his bride.

The air was thick in the church, burning Cooper's eyes and nose. He recognized this kind of smoke too well—it brought horrible old memories crashing over him. Parker held open the doors so Cooper could carry Tanya over the threshold and through the vestibule. Logan held open the doors to the outside while also trying to hold his mother from rushing back inside the church.

"We have to find the source of the fire," she said, tears streaming from her eyes. It probably wasn't just the smoke making her cry but fear for the chapel she had already fought so hard to save once. "We have to put it out—it'll take too long for the fire engines to arrive."

Cooper shook his head. "There is no fire."

Mom stared hopefully up at him. "But all the smoke…"

"There're no flames," he pointed out. "No heat."

"So what is it?" Logan asked as he coughed and his eyes streamed tears. This wasn't the kind of man who cried. He hadn't even cried as a kid—not even when their dad died. He had stayed strong for all of them.

"Tear gas," Cooper said. His eyes stung but stayed dry. He was used to this stuff—to chemical attacks used to flush soldiers out into an ambush. He peered outside and ordered his family, "Get back in here. The shooter could be out there."

But right now gunfire was the least of his concerns. He glanced down at his bride lying in his arms. She hadn't just passed out from fear. She was too still for that—too lifeless. "She's not breathing!" he realized, his heart slamming into his ribs.

"The gas must have aggravated her asthma," her sister said.

And he remembered the attacks she'd had in their youth, like at the site of the bonfire when she'd struggled for breath. "Get her inhaler!"

"She always has one in her purse," Rochelle replied. Finally showing some concern for her sister, she ran toward the bride's dressing room. But she returned moments later clutching Tanya's open bag. "It's not here."

Someone had set off the smoke bomb and stolen Tanya's inhaler. This person knew her well—too well. He put aside his suspicions for the moment to focus on his bride, though. He dropped to knees in the vestibule and began CPR. Pressing his lips to hers, he tried breathing for her—tried to give her his breath to bring her back.

"I'm calling 911," Logan said as he pulled his cell phone from his pocket.

But Cooper knew it would be too late. By the time the ambulance arrived, Tanya would have been deprived of oxygen for too long.

"Unless someone took it, too, I have something," his mother murmured. She pushed past her eldest son and hurried back into the church, disappearing down the stairwell to the basement banquet area, kitchen and offices.

"I hear sirens," Nikki said. "Someone must have reported the smoke."

Rochelle began to cry. "She's not breathing. She's not breathing…"

Footsteps pounded on the steps as his mother ran back up the stairs. "I have her extra inhaler," she said. "When we were planning the wedding, I made sure she brought a spare in case she forgot to bring hers on her wedding day."

Cooper grabbed it from her and pressed it to Tanya's open lips. She wouldn't be able to breathe it in—would it get through her compromised airway? Would it reduce the swelling?

He pushed it down so that it produced a puff of medicine. But most of it escaped her open mouth. He did it again. But there was no response. Her eyelids didn't so much as flicker, and she didn't breathe.

Had he already lost his wife?

EVERYTHING WAS DARK, as if Tanya had dropped into a black hole. But then awareness crept in—first with sound.

She could hear the beeping and buzzing of machines. The squeak of wheels on linoleum. And voices…

"She should have not been exposed to that gas," a man said, his tone chastising, "You're lucky her inhaler worked."

"I wasn't sure that it would. She was already unconscious." This voice she recognized as her husband's. But was Cooper actually her husband? She dimly remembered the minister pronouncing them man and wife. Then Cooper had swept her up in his arms.

Or had that all just been part of her fantasy?

Was any of it real?

"And she's still unconscious," Cooper continued.

"But she's breathing."

"Was the inhaler enough?" Cooper asked, his voice gruff with obvious concern. "Is she going to be all right?"

If not for the beeps and buzzes, Tanya would have thought she'd slipped into unconsciousness again. Because the man paused that long before replying, "We'll know when she awakens…"

"When?" Cooper asked hopefully. "Or *if…?*"

She was already awake. Her eyes were just too heavy to open, and her throat too dry and achy to speak. She struggled to move her fingers, but she was so weak, her muscles so leaden and appendages so heavy.

"I'm sorry," the man said. "I don't know…"

Since she hadn't recognized his voice, she'd just assumed he was a doctor. But maybe not…or he would realize that she was going to be fine.

She had to be fine.

A big hand closed over the fingers she struggled to move. And as he had in the church, he squeezed as if prodding her again. "Come on, Tanya, wake up…"

She tried again to raise her lids, but they were so

heavy. The effort exhausted her, but she gained a small space, enough that some light filtered between her lashes. She was fighting back the blackness.

But she wasn't fighting alone. Cooper held tightly to her hand as if pulling her back to him. "Come on, you're too tough to let this damn coward beat you…"

She had to be strong—not just for herself but for Stephen. She couldn't take a ransom call if she wasn't conscious. Then Cooper marrying her would have been for naught. She had to assure him that wasn't the case, so she concentrated on her fingers and managed to move them within his tight grasp.

He gasped. "Tanya? Can you hear me?"

She bent her fingers again, wriggling them. Then she managed, finally, to open her eyes.

"You're awake!"

She nodded weakly. And then, after licking her dry and cracked lips, she tried to speak. "Is—is…"

"Don't hurt your throat," he advised. "Just rest."

She shook her head now, which caused a wave of dizziness that threatened a return of unconsciousness. "Is everyone…okay?"

If his mother's Little White Wedding Chapel had been destroyed, she would never forgive herself. "Did the fire…"

"There was no fire," he said.

"But the smoke…" She coughed, just remembering it, as her airway and lungs ached.

"It wasn't a fire," he assured her with another squeeze of her fingers. "Someone opened a tear-gas canister in the church."

She coughed again. "Was anyone else…"

He shook his head. "No one else was hurt. Only you…"

"My asthma…" It didn't often flare up. But when it

did… Remembering his conversation with the man who must have been the doctor, she asked, "You found my inhaler in my purse?"

"There wasn't one in your purse, but Mom had gotten a spare from you earlier."

She'd seen the inhaler and the EpiPen for her peanut allergy when she'd taken her makeup bag out of her purse. "But it was there earlier…"

"Not when you needed it."

Someone hadn't opened the tear-gas canister just to stop the wedding. He or she had been trying to kill her. Her eyes stung and not from that smoke. She blinked hard, but the moisture leaked out.

The thin mattress depressed as Cooper joined her on the bed. Sitting down beside her, he pulled her into his arms, lifting her away from the pillows and the bed. "It's okay. You're safe now."

"You found out who's been doing this?"

He uttered a heavy sigh. "No, but we will. We'll find out."

She shivered as cool air blew in the back of her gown. And she touched the rough cotton. "Your mom's dress— is it okay?"

If they'd cut her out of it—if they'd destroyed it, it would have been as big a tragedy as the church burning down.

"It's fine," he assured her. "You need to stop worrying about everything and get some rest."

"I need to get out of here." She was definitely in a hospital, and not just in a curtained-off area of the emergency room. She had been admitted.

"You're too weak," he said.

"You said I was tough," she reminded him.

"You are—it's a miracle you survived at all. You

weren't breathing for so long." He shuddered now. "For too long…"

She managed to lift her hand to her head, which still felt too light—too hazy—as if she were still trying to see through the veil. She was tired. Weak…

Tears burned again, but she managed to blink them back this time. She had to be strong…enough to leave. "But if they call…"

"Logan has your phone," Cooper said. "He'll take the call."

"They might hang up…if they don't hear me…" And then what would happen to Stephen? He had already been hurt—that blood had to have been his. There'd been no one else in the groom's dressing room. "I need my…"

"Real groom," Cooper finished for her.

Incorrectly. She just needed her phone. And Cooper. But he was pulling back and standing up.

"We'll find him," he assured her. "We're all working on finding him."

Just then a knocking sounded and the door creaked open. "Is she awake? Is she all right?" a woman asked, her voice soft with concern.

"Yes," Tanya answered Cooper's sister. She was touched by the younger woman's concern but also disappointed that her own sister hadn't come to check on her. How had their relationship fallen apart so badly? "I'm fine."

Nikki's brown eyes, so like her mother's, warmed with affection and relief. "I'm so glad. You gave us quite the scare—some of us more than others, though." She glanced at her brother, as if checking to see if he'd recovered from that scare.

But Tanya doubted he had been very shaken. After surviving a war zone and returning home, the man had been shot at—twice—and hadn't lost his composure or his temper. He was unflappable.

"Is your mother okay?" Tanya asked.

"Worried about you," Nikki said. "But she's fine. Mom's the toughest woman I know."

Tanya suspected her daughter was tougher than she knew. "Your mom isn't the only one."

"She's not," Nikki agreed. "You're pretty tough, yourself. None of us thought you were going to make it."

If that was the truth, where was Rochelle? Didn't she care about her older sister at all? Tanya sighed, too, and shook off the self-pity. A relationship took two people to make it work. Maybe she had never tried hard enough with Rochelle. She'd been so busy with work and with trying not to think about Cooper. With trying not to worry about Cooper being deployed. With trying not to miss Cooper...

"She has no clue how close she came to not making it," Cooper said. "Even now she's more worried about Mom and Stephen and everyone else than she is herself. She needs to get some rest."

"She needs you to stop talking about her like she's not here," Tanya said, annoyed that he thought her so weak and more annoyed that she was so weak right now. At least physically...

Nikki laughed. "I forgot how long you two have been friends."

So had Tanya. But in her mind, they had never been just friends, even though she'd agreed with Cooper that that was all they'd been.

"You both act like an old married couple already," Nikki continued, "and it's only been a few hours since the wedding from hell—" She squeaked, as if wishing back her words, and her eyes widened in shock. "I'm sorry—"

Tanya had spent too much time around the Paynes not to know that this was how they dealt with every situation—with humor. And she was touched that she'd been included in that teasing.

"No, it definitely was the wedding from hell," Tanya agreed. The smoke had made her think she was in hell. Even now her throat still burned—her lungs still ached.

"I—I shouldn't have called it that," Nikki said, clearly embarrassed. "Mom would kill me."

At least Nikki would know who was trying. Tanya had no idea who wanted her dead. But she had to ask, "Have you found out anything about what happened at the church?"

Nikki opened her mouth, but Cooper shook his head. "You nearly died at the church," he said. "You need to rest if you're going to fully recover."

Tanya shook her head in denial. But her vision blurred with black spots as oblivion threatened to claim her again. She wouldn't admit it, but he was right. Exhaustion was overwhelming her, making her lids so heavy that she couldn't keep her eyes open any longer. Maybe if she closed them for just a moment…

His deep voice dropping to a whisper, Cooper said, "Let's let her sleep." The door creaked open as he ushered his sister into the hall.

Was that why he wanted to leave—so she could rest? Or because he didn't want her to hear whatever he was about to discuss with his sister? She tried to swing her legs over the bed, tried to sit up, but her legs were too heavy to move. And she couldn't lift her head from the pillow, let alone her torso, from the bed. The effort exhausted her completely so that she settled more heavily against the pillows. And sleep claimed her.

She had no idea how long she'd been out before the

door creaked open again. It couldn't have been that long, though, because she was still exhausted.

"That was fast…" she murmured sleepily. Nikki must not have had much to tell him. "I hope you didn't hurry on my account…"

He hadn't had to rush back to her bedside. It wasn't as if he were really her husband. Well, maybe he was really her husband—legally—but not emotionally. He wasn't in love with her. He hadn't actually wanted to marry her at all.

If not for Stephen…

"Did you find Stephen?" she asked.

Still he said nothing…

She fought to drag her eyes open again, but she only managed a little crack—just enough that she could peer between her lashes. And see the pillow coming toward her face.

She couldn't see who held the pillow—it blocked his or her face as it headed toward Tanya's. But she could see that the person wore scrubs. A member of the hospital staff? Or just someone posing as an employee?

Tanya lifted her arms to fend off the pillow. And she opened her mouth to scream. But she was still too weak—too weak to fight off her attacker—too weak to scream before the pillow covered her face and cut off her breath as effectively as the tear gas had.

She couldn't count on her new husband to save her again. She had to find the strength to save herself. Or die trying…

Chapter Ten

Wedding from hell.

Tanya had agreed with Nikki's assessment. Why? Because of the tear gas? Or because she hadn't married the groom she'd wanted—the one she loved?

"Has anyone found Stephen?" Cooper impatiently asked Nikki before they'd even walked far enough from Tanya's room so she wouldn't overhear them. Not that she would...

She was completely exhausted. He shuddered again as he remembered how close he had come to losing her.

Nikki shook her head.

"What about his computer?" he asked. "Did you find anything on it?"

Nikki's gaze dropped from his and she stared at the floor. She still wore her bridesmaid dress—that long bronze satin that made her look taller and older than he'd realized she was. Maybe it was the dress, but Cooper finally realized that his little sister had grown up. He'd been gone so long that he'd kept thinking of her as the child she'd been when he'd left. But she was a woman now.

Men in the hallway stared at her as they passed—until Cooper glared at them. Then they hurried along. Nikki didn't notice their interest though as she continued to ignore his question.

"What did you find?" he prodded her.

"She drunk emails like she drunk dials," Nikki spoke tentatively as if trying to purposely be vague. "I'm sure it didn't mean anything."

Because this was Nikki and not Logan or Parker, he held on to his patience and calmly asked, "What didn't mean anything—an email? You got into Stephen's email?"

Nikki bit her lip and nodded.

Not only had his little sister grown up but she'd acquired some serious skills, too. That computer had hit the asphalt hard the night before.

"What did you find?" he asked again. His patience had slipped away. He didn't want to leave Tanya alone for very long. But then, she wasn't alone as he had noticed someone in scrubs slip inside her room. Probably the nurse checking on her again…

Or the doctor…

He needed to check on her again himself—to make certain she was all right. Because he had that niggling feeling in the pit of his stomach as he had right before Parker had stepped into the line of fire at Stephen's condo complex.

"C'mon, Nikki!" he prodded her again—more forcefully.

"Rochelle sent Stephen some emails."

"Some?"

She nodded.

"I know she's your friend." Though he couldn't fathom why. "But you need to be straight with me."

"She was begging him not to marry Tanya."

He wasn't surprised. It was obvious that Rochelle was

against her sister's marrying Stephen even though she had showed up at the church for the wedding. Of course, Tanya hadn't married Stephen, though. She had married him. His heart slammed into his ribs as the truth fully sank in—he was married.

To Tanya…

But he wasn't the groom she'd wanted. That man was missing.

"She'd written more than that in those emails," he surmised.

Nikki grimaced and replied, "She said that if he left Tanya at the altar and married her instead, he would get all the inheritance instead of just half."

That niggling feeling intensified until Cooper grimaced from the force of it.

"Rochelle would probably be so embarrassed that I saw those," Nikki said. "And especially that I told you. She must have been drinking when she sent those emails…"

"Was she drunk or greedy?" Cooper asked. "Does she want the money all for herself?"

"I didn't think she wanted her grandfather's money at all," Nikki said. "She hated the old man so much."

"Maybe it's not the money she wants," Cooper said. "Maybe it's the man."

"So you think she's using the money to lure Stephen away from Tanya?" Nikki asked. Then, shaking her head, she added, "Never thought I would be happy I had brothers instead of sisters…"

"She's your friend," Cooper reminded her.

Nikki sighed. "I always felt sorry for her growing up in Tanya's shadow."

"What do you mean?"

"You don't know?" Nikki asked in astonishment. "And she's your wife."

"Only because Stephen disappeared." Or had he really?

"But you always had a crush on her," Nikki said. "All the guys did. She's beautiful and sweet and smart. It must have been hell having her for an older sister."

"So how much does Rochelle resent her?" he asked. "Enough to try to kill her?"

Nikki gasped. "Rochelle can be a brat sometimes, but she's not a killer."

"What about Stephen?"

"She would *never* hurt him," Nikki said. "Like you had the crush on Tanya, she's always had a crush on Stephen."

"She has the two greatest motives," Cooper pointed out. "Love and money."

Her lips curved into a teasing smile. "Well, I know which one motivated you…"

"Motivated me for what?" Did she think him responsible for Stephen's disappearance?

"To marry Tanya Chesterfield."

"I work for Payne Protection now," Cooper reminded her. "I only want to keep her safe." But that niggling sensation told him something was wrong. He turned back toward Tanya's room. Why hadn't the person in scrubs come back out?

"What's wrong?" Nikki asked.

But he was already heading back down the hall. As he approached the room, he heard a clang as something fell over and then that all-too-familiar sound of Tanya's scream. Fear for her safety overwhelmed him. "Call security!" he yelled at Nikki. He was reaching for the door when it banged open and that figure in scrubs came running out.

The person wore a surgical cap and face mask. Cooper would have reached for him, but the person also carried a gun, the barrel pointed at his chest. But he didn't fire. Instead, he kept running.

Nikki turned as if to follow, but Cooper caught her arm and tugged her inside the room with him. "Call security," he repeated. "Call Logan…"

Even as he barked those orders, his attention was on the woman in the bed. Or half out of the bed. The sheets had tangled around her, trapping her legs so that she hadn't been able to free herself.

She had been at the mercy of a madman while he'd been talking in the hall. He had failed to protect her. Again. Some husband he was proving to be; no wonder he had never intended to marry.

"Are you all right?" he asked.

Her face was flushed, but she was breathing—in pants and gasps.

"Call the doctor!" he yelled that order at his sister now.

Nikki, her eyes wide with shock and concern, hurried from the room to do his bidding.

Tanya clutched at his arms. "I—I fought him off."

"Yes, you did," he said, his chest swelling with pride that she had rallied her strength after having come so close to death just hours before. But then, she'd been fighting for her life, and he knew the fear of death could bring on a miraculous surge of strength.

"He—he tried to smother me…"

That explained the pillow on the floor. "He had a gun," he told her—no doubt the gun that had already fired so many shots at them.

She shuddered. "Why didn't he just shoot me?"

"Maybe he wanted it to look like you just stopped breathing again," he said. "And he didn't want anyone to hear the gunshot and catch him." He should have chased after him. But when Tanya screamed, he had to make certain she was all right. His heart hadn't stopped furiously pounding with his concern for her.

Tears glinted in her eyes. "Will he ever get caught?" she asked. "Will this ever be over?"

He silently cursed himself for not reaching for that mask. But with the gun pointed at his chest, he may have not lived to identify his killer. "Did you get a look at his face?"

The tears brimmed on her bottom lashes before spilling over onto her face. "No…"

Would she have let herself recognize her attacker if it was the person Cooper had begun to suspect? Would she be able to face the reality that someone she loved wanted her dead?

He wasn't sure he could accept it.

"That's fine," he assured her. "We'll catch him." Or die trying…

"I did something else, though," she said, and she lifted her hands from the sleeves of Cooper's tux to hold them up.

Blood smeared her fingers.

"You scratched him?" He hadn't seen any marks around the mask, but that had covered nearly all of the attacker's face.

She nodded. "I only got his arms…"

He whistled in appreciation of her strength and ingenuity. "You also got his DNA." And a definite conviction once Payne Protection tracked down the would-be killer. "That's my girl..."

THAT'S MY GIRL...

He had said that, but Cooper had yet to act as if Tanya was his girl. He wasn't even acting as if she was his wife, and they were on their honeymoon. They had spent the first night of that in the hospital. Cooper had stayed with her, but she didn't mistake his vigilance for love.

He wasn't acting like a husband; he was acting like a bodyguard. Instead of carrying her over the threshold of their hotel suite, he carried a gun and peered around him. "You'll be safe here," he assured her. "Nobody followed *us* from the hospital."

"What if they followed the others?" she asked.

"Then the plan worked."

The plan had consisted of Logan leaving the hospital with one of his female employees, who had worn a blond wig. And Parker had left with Nikki, who had also been wearing a blond wig. Since each of the men had worn the same ball cap, they had looked nearly identical except to her. Cooper was the most muscular and handsome. But someone else might have been fooled.

"Will they be safe?" She didn't want anyone else getting hurt because of her.

"They're all bodyguards," Cooper reminded her. "Since it's our job to protect others, we should certainly be able to protect ourselves."

He could. But, as a Marine, he had training that the others didn't have.

"You're not worried about them?" she asked.

A muscle twitched along his tightly clenched jaw. "It's not my job to worry about them."

But he clearly was.

"It's my job to worry about you," he said.

That was what she really was to him. Not his girl. Not his bride or wife. Not even his friend. She was just a job.

Maybe she wasn't as recovered from her asthma attack as she'd convinced the doctor, because she was suddenly so weary she dropped heavily onto the couch.

"You just told me I was safe here," she reminded him.

He had driven such a circuitous route to the hotel that *she* wasn't even certain where they were. But when they'd driven up, she had seen sunlight glinting off water and realized they were close to Lake Michigan. She would have stood up now and looked out the window to see if they had a lake view, but after what had happened last time, she didn't dare risk it.

"You're safe." He dropped onto the couch beside her and skimmed his knuckles across her cheek. "But I'm still worried about you. You've been through a lot the past couple of days."

She would have brought up that his mother might have been right about her wedding superstitions, but then she would have been bringing up the kiss that had happened when they'd been alone in a hotel room, like now.

"The doctor signed my release," she said. "I'm fine."

He studied her face as if he doubted the doctor's opinion. Did she look that bad? Nikki had brought her makeup, which Tanya had used to cover the dark circles beneath her eyes. But maybe she should have left the circles since they had been the only color in her very pale face.

Nikki had also brought the suitcase she'd packed for the honeymoon. But given that she and Stephen were only friends, her honeymoon clothes were more comfortable than sexy. She wore dark jeans with a green sweater.

Cooper also wore jeans, ones so faded and worn that

they clung to his muscular thighs, and a black sweater that clung to his muscular chest. He had ditched the cap and his black jacket before joining her on the couch.

"You're fine," he finally agreed. "Physically…"

She nodded, and his hand fell away from her face. But she could still feel his touch. Her skin tingled and her pulse raced with his closeness.

He continued, "But emotionally…"

Had he realized that she was falling for him? Was he about to give her the just-friends speech again?

"I am emotional," she admitted, embarrassed when she remembered how often she had cried in front of him just over the past couple of days. "But it's because I'm worried. About Stephen. About your family."

And, most especially, you…

But if she admitted that, he would know for certain that she'd fallen for him. And he would probably not only be appalled but offended that she didn't think him capable of protecting himself and her.

"And I'm worried about how naive you are," he said. "And how badly you're going to be disillusioned because of that…"

"Naive?" She laughed in amazement that she had been accused of that twice in as many days. "You think I'm naive? I'm a supervisor at the Department of Social Services for the second-biggest city in Michigan. I wouldn't have lasted a week on the job if I was naive or easily disillusioned." Her laughter turned into a heavy sigh. "In fact, I'm realistic enough to believe that somebody from one of those cases I've handled may be stalking me."

"It's gone beyond stalking," he bitterly reminded her.

She flinched. "Yes, Stephen was abducted."

"Someone's trying to kill *you*," he said. "And that person very nearly succeeded."

And he seemed more worried about her than Stephen.

"It could be someone who got angry over how I do my job," she said. She'd had to make some very unpopular decisions over the past several years.

He shook his head.

"You don't believe that." She studied his face now as intently as he had studied hers moments ago. "You've been acting strangely, like you have some idea who the culprit is. Do you?"

He just held her stare, his gaze locked on hers. Despite the brightness of the blue, there was also darkness in his eyes—as if the tragedy he'd witnessed was still there, haunting him. "I have my suspicions."

"Why won't you share them with me?" They were husband and wife—weren't they supposed to share everything? But they hadn't even shared a kiss yet to seal their union.

"I'm not sure you can handle it," he admitted as if she was some fragile female needing his protection.

While she did need his protection, she wasn't fragile. "I've been through a lot in the past couple of days." She smiled ruefully. "Certainly nothing like you've been through when you were deployed, but—"

He pressed a finger over her lips as if to block her from putting her foot any further into her mouth. But he was smiling ruefully, too. "You're tough," he said. "You've handled getting almost run down and shot at, smoked out and smothered…"

She shivered as he trailed off because she realized he considered this worse than all those things. Then she drew in a deep breath and asked, "Who?"

"You think this is about revenge for something you did or didn't do on your job."

Against her better judgment, she'd given him a list

of names. But she suspected he had not pursued any of those leads. "And you don't think so?"

He shook his head. "I think it's about the money."

"That's why I needed it to pay the ransom."

"What ransom?" he asked. "There's been no ransom demand."

Once she'd gotten her phone back from Logan, she'd kept it in her pocket. It hadn't rung. Her stomach churned. "That's not good for Stephen…"

"No, it's not," Cooper agreed.

"You think he's dead?" If he was, she might as well have murdered him herself—since she was the reason he'd died. "That's why they haven't called?"

He said nothing, just stared at her as if debating the wisdom of sharing his suspicions.

Pain clutched her heart. She needed to know if Stephen was dead. "Cooper?"

"I think they haven't called because Stephen can't make his own ransom call."

Maybe she wasn't as recovered as she'd thought, but she couldn't fathom what he was telling her. "What?"

"I think it's Stephen," he explained himself. "I think Stephen's trying to kill you."

The best friend she'd ever had? She laughed at the ludicrous thought of Stephen betraying her. Because if Cooper was right, Stephen didn't have to shoot or smother her. The betrayal alone would kill her.

Chapter Eleven

Did her laughter have an edge of hysteria to it? Had his admission struck her too hard?

Cooper studied her face for signs of distress. But he saw only the beauty of her flushed skin and sparkling green eyes. She had always distracted him. Maybe he wouldn't have had so much trouble in school if she hadn't been in so many of his classes.

"You don't believe Stephen could do this." Did she love him that much that she couldn't see him for the man he must have become?

"I would sooner believe *you* were trying to kill me."

He sucked in a breath, as stung as if she'd physically slapped him. "You could actually believe that I would try to kill you?"

"You've been gone a long time," she reminded him. "I don't know you anymore. I know Stephen. We've stayed friends all these years."

"Obviously you've been more than friends," Cooper said, trying to keep any bitterness from slipping into his voice. He had chosen to leave; what they'd done in his absence was none of his business. And it wouldn't have been even if he'd stayed.

But now Tanya was *his* wife. So she was his business.

Tanya's face flushed an even brighter shade of red. But all she said was, "Stephen has always been there for me."

"Until the wedding."

"That wasn't his fault."

"I'm not so sure about that," Cooper said.

Her brow furrowed with confusion. "How can you think that? You saw the blood. The signs of a struggle."

"If there was really a struggle, why didn't you or Mom hear it?"

She jumped up from the couch as if unable to sit still for his accusations. While she paced the small space in the living room of the suite, she kept her distance from the window. She obviously didn't feel safe.

And she wouldn't until they'd caught whoever was trying to kill her. But in order to do that they had to consider all the viable suspects.

"Your mom was in the basement," she reminded him, "talking to the minister. And I was in the bride's dressing room, way on the other side of the church. Someone must have hit him in the head while he was distracted and knocked him out in the groom's dressing room. That's why we didn't hear anything."

"We don't even know yet if the blood that was found is his," Cooper reminded her. DNA results didn't come back as quickly as they did on television shows.

"Now you're saying he hurt someone else?"

If Cooper was right, Stephen had hurt *her*—physically— a few times. And now emotionally...

"It might be his blood," Cooper amended. "But he could have drawn some earlier and sprayed it around the room."

She shuddered at the gruesome idea. "Why would he do that?"

"So you would think he was dead or hurt..." And

then she wouldn't marry, forfeiting her inheritance to her sister.

Obviously still in denial, she shook her head. "He wouldn't do that. It wouldn't even occur to Stephen to do something like that."

"He might not have been acting alone," Cooper pointed out.

She stopped in her tracks and stared at him. "Do you think he hired someone?"

"I don't think he had to hire someone."

"Someone was willing to help him?" She stared at Cooper for a few moments and sighed. "You already have someone in mind? Who?"

"Your sister."

"Rochelle?" She didn't laugh the way she had when he'd suggested Stephen might be behind the attempts on her life. But her brow furrowed again, this time in consideration, and she asked, "Do you think she hates me that much?"

He shrugged. "I don't know Rochelle. Like you said, I've been gone a long time. I feel as if I barely know Nikki—she was so young when I left."

"Nikki adores you," Tanya assured him. "Rochelle doesn't adore me. She can't stand me." Her voice heavy with resignation, she admitted, "She just might hate me enough to try to ruin my wedding. But Stephen would never work with her to hurt me."

Cooper had worried about telling her what he'd learned. He hadn't wanted to hurt her, too. So he hesitated.

But, of course, she noticed. She stared at him through narrowed eyes. "You found something that made you suspicious of them."

He shrugged. "Maybe I'm just suspicious of everyone."

She nodded. "Yes, you've changed. You're not the boy I used to know. You're cynical now."

He had reason to be. As a teenager who'd lost his dad, he'd had reason to be. "Everybody grows up and changes."

"I'm not so sure about Rochelle," she ruefully admitted. "But if you're trying to tell me that Stephen's changed…". She shook her head. "I know him too well."

"Did he tell you about all the emails Rochelle sent him?"

She tensed, as if his words had struck her.

"So he didn't tell you…"

She shrugged. "That doesn't mean he was hiding them," she defended Stephen. "Maybe he didn't want to cause any more trouble between me and Rochelle. I can't imagine those emails were telling him how lucky he was to be marrying me."

"No," he replied. "She didn't want him to marry you at all. She wanted him to marry her—for *all* the money."

She laughed. "And that's why you think they're working together?"

"All is more than half," he pointed out. "It's powerful motivation."

"Not for Stephen. He doesn't care about the money."

"Everybody cares about money—especially *that* amount of money." Given how wealthy her grandfather had been, her inheritance had to be millions—maybe even billions.

"Grandfather's lawyer told me that you care about the money, so much that you may have gotten Stephen out of the way so you could marry me yourself."

He flinched with a little twinge of guilt. He had been jealous of Stephen marrying her but not so petty that he would have wished harm come to him. He had considered Stephen his friend before he'd begun to consider him a suspect.

She laughed. "But I assured Mr. Gregory that you really didn't want to marry me at all—that's why I didn't let him bring that prenup to you."

"You should have let him," he said. "I would have signed it." And he really wished he had. He didn't want her doubting him. It wouldn't be easy to keep her safe if she didn't trust him.

"I was worried that you might be offended."

"That he thinks I want your money? Or that he thought I got rid of Stephen to get it?" Apparently, Arthur Gregory thought even less of Cooper than his employer had. He shrugged off the man's accusation; he didn't care what anyone—except Tanya—thought of him.

She laughed again but nervously this time. "He didn't think the money was your only reason."

"What other reason would I have?" Stephen had always been a good friend to him. He'd even tried to stay in touch after Cooper had gone away. But Cooper had been determined to put his past behind him and move on from his loss—of his dad and of Tanya. But by doing that he'd almost lost more—his family and his life.

"Me." She laughed again with self-deprecation. "He thinks you always had a crush on me."

If he wanted her to trust him, he had to be straight with her. "I did."

But if he was being completely honest, he shouldn't have used the past tense. Because he definitely still had a crush on her—one so big that he maybe should have even called it *love*.

GIDDINESS RUSHED OVER Tanya, so that her breath quickened and her pulse raced and her head grew light. Maybe she wasn't completely recovered from the asthma attack. Or maybe she was still that teenage girl who had been madly in love with Cooper Payne.

But that love had been crushed years ago—when Cooper had insisted they were just friends. "If he was right about that," she said, "was he right about my grandfather warning you to stay away from me?"

He sighed and nodded.

And hope flared that maybe he had shared all those feelings she'd had for him.

But then he spoke. "He was right, though. We had nothing in common then. You were going off to college and I was going off to the Marines. Maybe it was smarter to never get involved than to get involved and break up."

"Why would we have broken up?" she asked. She never would have broken up with him. She would have written him letters daily. She would have waited for him to come home to her. Maybe she had waited anyway— since she'd never fallen for another man the way she'd fallen for the boy he'd been.

"We had nothing in common then," he repeated. "And we have even less in common now."

"Are you sure about that?" she asked. "You want to protect people—as a Marine and now as a bodyguard. I want to protect people, too." That was why she'd wanted her inheritance—to help more families than the state's limited budget allowed her to help.

"As a social worker, you do protect them," he said. "I'm actually surprised your grandfather didn't talk you into pursuing a different career."

"He tried," she admitted. "But I wasn't as easy to manipulate as you must have been."

He scowled as if she'd insulted him. And then he laughed. "Your grandfather didn't manipulate me."

"He got his way," she said. "Just like he's getting his way now—getting me to marry for his money."

Cooper laughed again. "I was the last person he wanted you to marry, so he's definitely not getting his way."

"Mr. Gregory said that Grandfather would haunt him if he'd walked me down the aisle to you." She sighed. "I sometimes wonder if he's haunting me now, with all that's happened—the threats, Stephen's disappearance…"

His mouth curved into a small grin. "You think a ghost is responsible for all this?"

"I'd rather blame a ghost than myself."

"None of this is your fault," he assured her.

"You want me to believe its Stephen's."

"And maybe Rochelle's, working together."

She shuddered. "I don't want to believe it's either of them."

"What about me?" he asked. "Do you want to believe it's me?"

She shook her head. "No."

Yet goose bumps lifted on her skin. What if it was him? What if Mr. Gregory had been right? And she was alone with the man who'd gotten rid of Stephen?

"I see your fear," he said. "You may not want to believe it, but you're worried that your grandfather's lawyer could be right about me." He reached inside his jacket where he kept his gun holstered. But he pulled out his phone instead. "I'll call one of my brothers to take my place."

"Don't," she said.

But he'd already pressed a button on his cell—probably the two-way feature. Instead of a voice emanating from the speaker, gunshots rang out. And he cursed. "Logan! Logan, damn it! Are you all right?"

"Go to him," she urged. "Make sure he's safe!"

Cooper shook his head. "I can't."

"You can leave me," she said. "I'll be safe. Or do what Logan did and leave me a gun."

"I can't go to Logan." Cooper brushed his hand over the top of his head before clenching his fingers into a fist of frustration. "Because he didn't tell me where he was going. Neither did Parker."

She was shocked. "You didn't trust each other?"

"We didn't want anyone to be coerced into revealing the other's location."

Like any of his family would have given up any of the others. They weren't like her and her sister. Rochelle had tried to talk her groom out of marrying her. Out of spite or greed?

"Logan!" he shouted into the phone.

The shots reverberated and then tires squealed. And Logan finally replied with a string of curses. "The weasel got away again."

"Did you see him?"

"Not his face," Logan griped. "Had a hat pulled low, sunglasses and his collar pulled up."

"Could it have been Stephen?"

"Same height and build," Logan replied. "Could've been…"

And for the first time Tanya realized it was a possibility that Stephen had turned on her—that he'd decided he wanted all the money. She was dimly aware of the rest of Cooper's conversation.

"Are you all right?" he asked his brother.

"Yeah, but the hotel will be pissed over the windows of our suite getting shot up."

"Seems to be this guy's M.O."

"Coward," Logan cursed him. "The police are coming. They probably won't be surprised to see *me* again…"

"Good luck," Cooper murmured before clicking off. "I'll call Parker."

"Wait!" she implored him. "It doesn't make sense that Stephen would do this. He has money."

"People with money never seem to think they have enough," Cooper replied. "Your grandfather was certainly never satisfied."

Not just with the size of his bank accounts but with his family either.

"But Stephen…" She shuddered. "It makes no sense, especially now. We're already married. Why keep trying to kill me?"

"If you listened to your lawyer, I'm probably doing it so I can collect your inheritance myself."

"But Rochelle could challenge you," she said, "since our marriage hasn't been consummated." Heat flushed her face that she'd brought up that idea—and an image in her head of Cooper. Naked.

"What?" he asked, his eyes dilating as if he had conjured an image of his own.

"She doesn't even have to kill me to collect her inheritance," Tanya realized. "All she has to do is wait until tomorrow and challenge our marriage."

"What do you mean?"

"If we don't consummate our wedding before my birthday, she could challenge its validity." Knowing Rochelle, she probably would anyway—just to be spiteful.

Cooper nodded as realization dawned on him. "And then she and Stephen can marry and collect it all?"

She hesitated, unwilling to believe that her best friend could have agreed to betray her. Then she sighed in resignation and replied, "Yes."

"We can lie," he said. "We can say that we consummated our marriage. How is she going to prove we're lying? Aren't you a good liar?"

She had never been until that day she'd agreed with him that they could have only ever been friends. He was the only one who had ever believed her lie. "According to my sister, no."

Because Rochelle hadn't believed that Tanya was in love with Stephen. She'd realized that she'd only intended to marry him to collect her inheritance.

"I would lie to Rochelle," she said. "But I couldn't lie to a judge if my sister challenges us in court. For my job I've had to testify a lot, and if it was ever proven that I committed perjury…" All those other cases could be called into question. It wasn't a risk she was willing to take.

"Then what do you intend to do?" he asked. "If I'm right about Stephen, you don't need to inherit to pay his ransom."

"There has been no demand…" Her groom had not been kidnapped. He could still be hurt, though. Or he could be out there shooting out windows and running down people with cars and tossing tear-gas canisters.

"So you don't need the money," he said.

But she did need the money. For all those people she wanted to help and for an even better reason now. "Then if you're right, Rochelle and Stephen will get it all."

"Not if we can prove what they've done."

"Can we prove it?" she asked. "Are those emails enough to bring any charges against them?"

"No," he admitted. "We would need more evidence."

"Evidence that we might never find," she said. "I work cases where I know there's neglect or abuse, but so many times I haven't been able to prove it." Until it was too late…

She blinked against the sting of tears.

And Cooper squeezed her shoulder. "You really care about your job, about those people…"

Too much to let Rochelle collect money that could help them.

"I care," she said. "Do you?"

"I want to protect you, Tanya."

She drew in a deep breath to gather her courage. "Then make love to me. Consummate our marriage."

Chapter Twelve

Make love to me.

He couldn't have heard her correctly. He must have been daydreaming. And his heart was only pounding as wildly as it was because of the shots he'd heard being fired at his eldest brother. It wasn't because he was hoping like hell that he had heard her *correctly*.

Desire rushed up, choking him, so that he had to clear his throat before asking, "What did you say?"

Her face flushed a bright shade of pink. Clearly too embarrassed to speak, she just shook her head.

Nobody had ever accused him of being too sensitive. Maybe he would have to learn some sensitivity—now that he was a married man and all. But he wasn't a really married man unless...

"You heard me," she challenged him.

"I heard you," he admitted. "But I don't understand you." If she was so in love with Stephen...

"I thought I'd made it clear," she said.

He shook his head now—trying to clear the passion from it, so he could think clearly.

"If Rochelle challenges this marriage in court," she said, "I won't perjure myself."

He wanted her. But he wanted her to want him, too,

as more than a means to an end. "So you want to sleep with me to spite your sister?"

"To stop her from getting what she wants," Tanya replied. "The money."

"And what about Stephen?" What were Tanya's feelings for her missing fiancé? She had been so loyal in her defense of him. Where was that loyalty now?

"If you're right and they're in on this together, she can have him!"

"*I* don't know what's right or wrong," Cooper admitted. "I was just saying it was a possibility that they could be in on it together."

"Because of the emails," she said with a nod.

She was as hurt as he had worried she would be if he shared his suspicions. But he'd had to be honest with her then. And now.

"But maybe they're not," he said. "We didn't find any reply to her email from Stephen. So maybe he has nothing to do with any of this." He actually hoped that was the case or he had lost a friend, too. But if Stephen wasn't in on it and had been seriously injured, Cooper may have already lost a friend. And then he'd married that friend's bride.

That made him the biggest betrayer.

Tears glistened in her eyes. "I don't know what I want to believe anymore. If he's working with Rochelle, at least he's alive. He's a snake," she cursed him, "but he's alive. If he's not working with her, where is he?"

"We're still looking for him," Cooper assured her. "Parker's in touch with all his old contacts from when he worked Vice." While Logan had quickly moved from patrol to detective, Parker had preferred working undercover. Or, if his reputation was to be believed, under *covers*.

Cooper would like to get under covers with his bride. But for the right reasons…

Like mutual desire. Need. Love…

"Vice?" she asked. "What would that have to do with Stephen?"

"Parker's informants are on the streets," he said. "They hear things. They see things." And hopefully one of their tips would lead them to Stephen. "And everyone on the Payne Protection payroll is working on finding him and whoever has been shooting at you."

"At you and your brothers, too," she reminded him. "I'm sorry—sorry for all the trouble I've been. I shouldn't have asked you to…"

"Make love to you?"

She flushed again. "I know it wouldn't have been making love. I know we're not really married."

"The minister pronounced us man and wife," he said. Had she been aware of that or had she already passed out?

"You made him do that before we left the church," she said, her head tilted as if she searched for the memories. "Everybody thought the building was on fire, but you made him finish the ceremony…"

"I recognized the kind of smoke," he said. "I didn't think we were really in danger. But then you stopped breathing…" He shuddered at his own memories of their ceremony and of holding her lifeless body in his arms.

"You saved me," she said. "Did I thank you for that?"

"I don't want your gratitude," he said.

He wanted *her*. Body, soul and heart. But no matter what the minister had pronounced them, she was not really his wife.

"I know you're just doing your job," she said. "But it's *my* life you keep saving…"

It was more than his job. She was more than his job.

And in saving her life, he was saving his own. Because without her…

"I can't ask you for anything else," she said, her face still flushed but downturned—as if she was unable to meet his gaze. "Forget what I said…"

It would be easier to forget his name than to forget what she'd suggested, what she'd asked him to do—with her.

Make love…

Tanya looked for a hole to crawl into, but despite her pacing, she hadn't worn one into the floor. So she glanced toward the door that led to the bedroom. But her face got even hotter with the embarrassment coursing through her. "I—I should probably…"

Unpack? She had so few things in her bag. Rest? She'd already slept more in the hospital than she had the past few months as she'd wrestled with the idea of marrying Stephen only for her money.

What wouldn't she do for that money?

She had asked Cooper to sleep with her. But had that been for the inheritance? Or was that just because she really, really wanted to sleep with her husband?

From the way her pulse raced and skin tingled, she suspected it was the latter, and she'd just used the money as an excuse.

"I—I just need to be alone for a little while," she admitted. Like maybe the rest of her life…

But when she headed toward that open bedroom door, he caught her wrist and stopped her in her tracks. "You can't leave yet."

"I'm just going into the other room…" The bedroom.

"You can't leave me yet," he said.

She turned back and chanced a glance at his face—his very handsome, very serious face. "It's not like I'm divorcing you," she teased, or attempted to, "I'm just leaving this room."

"You won't have to divorce me," he reminded her.

Because they hadn't consummated their marriage.

"The minister pronounced us man and wife," he continued, "but we never sealed it with a kiss."

"You want to kiss me?" she asked. But even as she turned up her face to ask the question, he was lowering his head. His lips brushed across hers in a nothing kiss— a mere whisper of breath and warmth.

Was that it? Was it over?

She wanted more. So she reached up, closed her hands around the nape of his neck and pulled his head down again. And she kissed him back.

The passion she'd had for him over a decade ago had been a young girl's passion. What she felt now was a woman's passion—hot and deep and overwhelming in its intensity.

She kissed him with all the heat burning inside her. First he was tense against her, but then he groaned. And his arms closed around her, pulling her up against him. Her breasts pushed against his chest.

And his tongue pushed against her lips before sliding between them, sliding over her tongue. Did he taste her desire? Did he know how much she wanted him?

She moaned as need overwhelmed her. But this was just a kiss…

The kiss that they should have had on their wedding day. But she had nearly died.

She had nearly lost this opportunity to kiss Cooper again. But she wanted so much more than his kiss…

So she moved her fingers from his nape down to his broad shoulders. Then she moved her hands lower, to press her palms against his chest. He tensed again, as if he expected her to push him back. But instead, she slid her hands over the impressive, rippling muscles of his chest. But his sweater separated her hands from his skin. So she reached for the waist of it and tugged it up, her knuckles skimming across the washboard muscles of his abs. He finished the job for her, first taking off his holster and gun and setting them onto the table next to the couch. Then he dragged the sweater over his head and dropped it onto the floor.

Damn. The man was hot. Figuratively and literally... so damn hot.

She burned up just from touching him.

Then he was touching her, too. His hands slid down her back to her waist. But he locked his hands around it and lifted her, swinging her up in his arms. He carried her into that room she'd wanted to go into—to be alone.

But when he dropped her onto the bed, she clung to him, unwilling to let him go. "Stay with me," she pleaded. She arched up and pressed a kiss to his lips, and another to his shoulder, and another to his chest, where his heart pounded furiously.

"Are you sure?" he asked.

In reply, she pulled off her sweater and shimmied out of her jeans. Maybe he'd already noticed when he'd gone through her apartment earlier that week that she had a thing for fancy underwear. She wore some now: a lacy red bra that barely contained her breasts and a matching thong.

He groaned again. "I hope to hell you're sure..."

"Very sure." And it wasn't about the money. Or the spite...

She wanted Cooper Payne because she had always wanted Cooper Payne. She opened her mouth to tell him, but he kissed her.

He kissed her passionately, his tongue sliding in and out of her mouth. And he touched her, sliding his hands over her stomach.

She sucked in a breath at the heat of his touch. And her skin tingled everywhere. She waited for his hands to move, to slide up, and finally they moved toward her breasts, tracing the underwire of her bra before undoing the delicate gold clasp between the cups. Her breath escaped in a gasp when he touched her breasts.

And her heart pounded madly.

She grabbed his arms to tug him onto the bed with her. But he pulled back.

She tensed, worried that he'd changed his mind, that he was about to say that he didn't want her. But he unsnapped his jeans and pushed them down and his underwear. And he proved he wanted her very much.

His erection jutted toward her. She reached for it. But he caught her hand and lifted it over her head. "Not yet," he said, "or this'll be over all too soon."

It must have been a while for him since he'd been deployed.

But instead of rushing, he took his time. He lifted both arms over her head, which had her breasts arching up as if begging for his touch.

He touched. First with his hands, caressing her skin. Then with his fingers, he teased her nipples.

Pressure built inside her, unbearable in its intensity. She squirmed on the bed, pushing her hips against his. That thin strip of lace separated her from his flesh. But it was already dampening with her desire for him.

Then he touched with his lips, skimming them over her skin before closing them around a nipple while he plucked at the other. She arched off the bed and moaned.

It had been a long time for her, too. She'd blamed her

lack of relationships on the threats. But now she knew… she'd been disappointed with every man she'd ever dated because he hadn't been Cooper.

She wasn't disappointed now.

He kissed her mouth while he moved his hand over her stomach. He pushed aside that scrap of lace and teased her with his fingers.

"Cooper…" She nearly sobbed his name as the pressure built to a new intensity. "Please…"

He kept kissing her, moving his mouth from her lips to her breasts. He teased her before moving his mouth even lower on her body. Finally he pulled off that thin strip of lace and tossed it onto the floor with the rest of their clothes.

She clutched at the sheets as he made love to her with his lips and tongue. And she screamed as sensations raced through her, releasing that intensity.

She was trembling. But she wasn't the only one, his arms shook a little as he braced them on the bed and covered her body with his. She reached between them and closed her hands around his erection. It was so smooth but hard and pulsing as if it had a life of its own. She parted her legs and guided him inside her, arching up as he thrust.

He was big—so big—that he stretched and filled her. But somehow they fit. Perfectly. She locked her arms and legs around him and matched his rhythm. They moved as one. The pressure building inside her she could feel in the tension in his body, the tightness of his muscles.

Cords extended in his neck. A vein in his forehead. And that muscle twitched along his jaw, as if his teeth were gritted. Still, a groan slipped out.

He reached between them and pressed his thumb to the most sensitive part of her. An orgasm shuddered through her body with such force that she screamed. She screamed and sobbed his name.

He joined her, pulsing and pumping inside her. And another groan tore from his throat with such force it would probably leave his voice hoarse. He collapsed on top of her.

She welcomed his weight and heat. She'd felt so alone and cold for so long. But then he rolled off her, taking away his warmth. And his body filled with tension again.

Was he already regretting what they'd done?

She had no regrets—except that it was already over. She wanted to do it again. She reached out a hand and touched his shoulder. "Cooper—"

He turned and pressed a hand over her mouth. "Listen…"

And then she heard it, too. Footsteps in the hall outside the hotel room door. First they passed. Then they stopped and turned back. And stopped again. Through the open bedroom door, she could see that a shadow fell from beneath the door to the hotel hallway.

And the knob of that outside door rattled.

His hand had slid away so she could speak, but she only risked a whisper. "You said nobody knows where we are…"

"Nobody does."

Obviously someone did. And they had come for them. For her…

The knob rattled again and they watched as the tumbler turned and the lock—unlocked.

Tanya wanted to scream again, but it was caught in her throat on the fear that was overwhelming her.

Chapter Thirteen

His gun was in the other room and his pants were on the floor. Some bodyguard Cooper had proved to be. But he let none of that distract him as he had let Tanya distract him. He vaulted out of the bed and grabbed for his gun in the living room of the suite. He managed to unholster and aim the barrel at the door as it opened.

He could have waited for the suspect to step inside, but if the shooter started firing wildly again, he might hit Tanya. Cooper hadn't shut the door between the bedroom and living area. But he couldn't see her. She had scrambled out of bed, hopefully to put on some clothes.

He hadn't had time.

"Come any closer and I'll blow your head off!" he threatened.

A laugh rang out; it was loud and grating and obnoxiously familiar. "Don't shoot your favorite brother!" Parker poked his head around the door and then he laughed again, more loudly, as he spied Cooper's nakedness.

"Get out!" he yelled at him.

"Okay, okay, I'll be waiting outside." Parker stepped back out and pulled the door closed.

"You told me they didn't know where you are," Tanya

said, her voice full of accusation and embarrassment. She was fully dressed now, while he stood naked before her.

"I didn't think they did…"

Had one of them followed him? Didn't they trust him? Then, given how badly he had just lost his objectivity, they were right not to trust him.

Cursing beneath his breath, he hurriedly grabbed up his clothes and pulled them on. Even though he knew it was Parker who'd broken in, he strapped on his holster and weapon, too, before stepping outside the hotel room.

Parker leaned against the wall opposite the door. He was still chuckling. "And they say *I'm* the playboy…"

Forcing the words out between gritted teeth, Cooper said, "I am not a playboy."

"That's right," Parker said. "You're a married man now."

Officially married now that they had consummated it.

"And you're a damn fool," he retorted. He wasn't just teasing now.

"A damn fool that tracked you down," Parker taunted him.

Guilt overwhelmed Cooper. He had failed to protect Tanya in every way. "How?"

"I have my sources."

"Have they turned up Stephen yet?" That would explain Parker's reason for tracking him down.

He shook his head. "No."

"Then why are you here? Did you just get bored?"

He laughed again. "Yeah, I didn't get sent undercover with a girl."

"Nikki's a girl."

"She's my sister," he said with great disgust.

"You two didn't get shot at?"

"*We* didn't get followed," he said with a huge grin. Logan wasn't about to live this one down.

"Neither did I," Cooper said. "So why'd you track me down and blow our hiding place? And a better question yet, why on earth did you pick the lock and open the door?" He had very nearly shot him.

"I heard the screaming," Parker said.

Heat climbed from Cooper's neck into his face. *He* was never going to live this one down. "Maybe you're not the playboy everyone thinks you are if you've never heard that kind of scream before…"

Parker punched his shoulder. "I've never had any complaints."

"At least you've dated polite women…"

Parker laughed again. "You're funny. I've forgotten how funny you can be."

So had Cooper. He'd left his family because they'd reminded him of his father—and his loss and the tragedy and grief. He'd forgotten the teasing and laughter. The fun. He'd lost that when he'd left.

But if he didn't find out who kept shooting at all of them, he risked losing that again. "Why are you here?" he asked. "Is Logan really all right? He didn't get hit?"

"Of course not. If it had been at all close, Candace would have jumped in front and taken the bullet for him."

It was no secret to anyone but Logan that one of his employees was hopelessly in love with him. Cooper had had to be back only a few days to figure it out.

"If Logan's fine, why are you here?"

Parker groaned. "Mom."

"Logan's letting her interfere in his business again?"

"She's Mom," he said as if that explained it all, and it actually did. "He was only appeasing her by saying that if I could find you, he'd have me bring you back."

"Why?"

"Because he thinks if I could find you, someone else could, too. However, he is completely underestimating my skills." But instead of being resentful like Nikki, Parker simply shrugged—unconcerned.

Logan wasn't the only one guilty of underestimating Parker; Cooper had, too. "He may be right..." Had he been gone so long that he didn't know the city as well as he once had? "How did you find me?"

"Figured you'd pick a nice place—it being your honeymoon and all." He smirked.

"And you have contacts here?"

"Higher-class contacts, but yeah."

"Where are we supposed to go now that you've blown this spot?"

"Back to the church."

"Like that place is safe..."

"Mom thinks it is—not because of the place but because we'll all be together. She thinks we're stronger that way than split up."

Given that Logan had just been shot at, Cooper couldn't argue her logic. If they had been together, someone would have been able to chase down the shooter while the one getting shot at took cover. "We can all be together, but we don't have to be at the church."

"Since the little tear-gas bomb changed her plans for yesterday, she wants to have your reception today," Parker explained.

"It's a little late for that."

"It's not too late for Tanya's birthday party."

"That's tomorrow," Cooper reminded them. She'd had to be married by that time in order to collect her inheritance. But not only did she have to be married, she'd had to consummate that marriage. Cooper had to remind himself that was the only reason they'd made love—for money.

Love had had nothing to do with it—at least not on her side.

"Mom doesn't think the food will last another day."

And given that Logan had just been shot at again, maybe he and Tanya wouldn't either.

SMOKE ROSE FROM the tiny flickering flames. Tanya closed her eyes to block out the fire. Then she expelled the breath she held and hoped that she'd blown them all out. All thirty of them. There had been enough room for all of the candles since it was her wedding cake Mrs. Payne had put out for her wedding reception/birthday party.

"Did you make a wish, dear?" the older woman asked.

Tanya opened her eyes and her gaze fell upon her husband. And she wished it was real.

Sure, they had consummated their marriage. But they hadn't made love. At least he hadn't.

She was in love. But she was in that alone.

She wasn't alone now. All of the Payne family and some of their employees had gathered in the high-ceilinged lower level of the Little White Wedding Chapel. It was a beautiful room with brocade wallpaper that looked like lace on the walls, and the coffered ceiling had built-in lights. Lights twinkled everywhere, making the space look like Wonderland. Even the floor had a sparkle to it—as if it had been sprinkled with fairy dust.

And she thought again, as she had when Mrs. Payne had produced that dress, that the older woman could be a fairy godmother. But Tanya was no Cinderella; she was unlikely to wind up with the prince.

"I wished that your dress is really okay," she replied.

Mrs. Payne shook her head in disappointment. "You're not supposed to tell what you wished for."

"Or it won't come true…"

"In this case, it's already true," Mrs. Payne said. "The dress is fine."

"They didn't cut it off?"

Mrs. Payne shook her head. "The paramedic was female. She understood the importance of your wedding dress."

"*Your* wedding dress." Tanya had only borrowed it because someone had maliciously destroyed hers. She glanced around the room until she located Rochelle. Why had she come to the party? To try to kill her again?

With all the Paynes and their associates in the room, she would be a fool to try anything here. But then, she'd been a fool to try anything at all. Had Tanya ever really known her younger sister?

Not like the Paynes knew each other.

She had overheard Cooper's conversation with Parker—their male ribbing. And she had worried that she would never be able to face the older Payne brother after what he had overheard. But when she'd stepped into the hall, he had acted as charming and friendly as he always had.

It was Cooper who acted differently. Or maybe it was that he acted the same, too, and she wanted him to be different with her. He still acted as if they were only old acquaintances. He didn't even act as if he was her friend, let alone her husband.

Her lover.

Disappointment tugged at the smile she'd pasted on when she'd stepped inside the reception hall.

"Now it's time to cut the cake," Mrs. Payne announced. "Cooper, get over here."

He'd had his head bent close to his brothers', as they huddled together in one corner of the room. They were all such beautiful men with that black hair and those eyes so bright a blue they glittered, like all those twinkling lights, even from across the room. Cooper's gaze met hers as he lifted his head.

And her heart clutched inside her chest, stealing her breath for a moment.

"No," she protested her unreciprocated feelings and Mrs. Payne's suggestion. "You can cut the cake. It's not like this is a real reception."

"Maybe it's more real than you're willing to admit," Mrs. Payne said with a little smile and a twinkle in her brown eyes.

Had Parker told her what he'd overheard?

Or had Tanya given herself away with how she couldn't stop looking at Cooper? But she didn't see him as he was now, dressed in his sweater and jeans; she saw him as he'd been in bed with her, gloriously naked and aroused. Wanting *her*...

Or after his last deployment, would any woman have done?

Mrs. Payne squeezed her shoulder. "It will all work out, honey."

How could she believe that—after how tragically she had lost her husband? She had to know that not all endings were happy.

Sometimes things just ended. Like her marriage to Cooper was destined to end—in divorce now since they would not be able to get an annulment after what they'd done that afternoon.

"What will all work out?" Cooper asked as he joined them, his blue eyes narrowed with suspicion.

Did he suspect, as she had come to suspect, that his mother was playing matchmaker for the two of them?

Mrs. Payne smiled and patted his cheek. "Don't worry so much, sweetheart."

"Easier said than done with a shooter on the loose…" He glanced in her sister's direction, too.

Tanya had never seen Rochelle with a gun. She doubted she would be able to fire one at all, let alone with any accuracy. And the night of the rehearsal, she'd been so drunk that Nikki had driven her home and stayed to make sure she was all right. She wouldn't have been able to try to run down Tanya with the car or to shoot out the window of her apartment. So, if she was behind the attempts, she was working with someone else.

Stephen?

The pain of betrayal struck her with a jolt. She didn't want to believe he would hurt her or anyone else. But who else could it be?

Someone from her job wouldn't have known about her inheritance. She had been very careful that no one had learned she was Benedict Bradford's granddaughter. So they would have had no reason to try to stop her wedding.

"You and your brothers will find out who's done all these horrible things," Mrs. Payne said to Cooper. "It's such a shame that the wedding was ruined. You should be in your tux and gown right now."

"But we're not, Mom," he pointed out. "So there's no reason to cut the cake or whatever other nonsense you have planned."

She gasped and pressed a hand to her heart as if her son had driven the knife she held into it. "Weddings are not nonsense. They are tradition. They are the foundation that needs to be laid for a long and happy marriage."

"Mom, you know I'm not the man Tanya was supposed to marry." And just as she'd said, he added, "This isn't real."

His mother, probably wisely, didn't share her cryptic comment with her son. Instead, she handed him the knife. "But it needs to look real." She glanced toward Rochelle, too, who had been joined by the lawyer. "People need to believe this is real…"

Would that bring Stephen back safely? Or was he the threat?

Once Cooper's hand closed around the handle of the knife, Mrs. Payne lifted Tanya's hand and placed it over his. And she squeezed, as if offering her blessing.

Her blessing wasn't what Tanya needed. It was Cooper's love. But his hand tensed beneath hers, as if he couldn't bear her touch.

Now.

He hadn't protested when she'd touched him back at the hotel. Or actually, he had protested—because he hadn't wanted her to rush their lovemaking. He had taken his time with her—kissing and caressing every inch of her.

Her skin flushed and tingled as she remembered how thoroughly he'd made love to her. He gazed down at her, and that glint in his eyes ignited to a hot spark, as if he was sharing those memories with her.

Her lips parted, and her breath escaped in a soft gasp. She wanted him to lean down and press his mouth to hers. She wanted his kiss.

She wanted him.

His hand tensed beneath hers, as if he felt the heat of her desire. Then he pushed the knife through the bottom layer of cake.

Desire heated her skin and blood, sending it racing fast and heavy through her veins. Would she ever not want him? Even here, in front of his family and what was left of hers, she couldn't control her passion for him.

He turned the blade of the knife to lift the cake. It was red velvet with cream-cheese frosting. She couldn't wait for a taste. With his fingers he broke off a smaller piece of the slice they'd cut together and held it to her lips. She opened her mouth and took a bite—carefully—so that her tongue managed to flick across his fingers. She preferred his taste to the cake's.

His pupils dilated and his nostrils flared as he dragged in a deep breath. "Tanya…"

She licked her lips slowly, sensually.

And Cooper groaned.

But then she realized what she tasted wasn't his fingers. Or red velvet cake and cream-cheese frosting. It was peanuts. Or peanut oil.

Didn't matter which one. Either one was dangerous enough to kill her. She didn't carry just an inhaler. She carried an EpiPen, too. But it hadn't been in her purse when Nikki brought it to her.

Now she knew why. Whoever was after her had not wanted her to have access to it after she was poisoned with peanuts. Her tongue felt thick and dry. And her throat was beginning to swell. She lifted her hands to her neck and gasped for breath.

Cooper had brought her back to life once. But she couldn't count on him doing it again. She couldn't count on anything. That was why she was glad they'd made love. Now she wished she'd told him that she loved him.

But she couldn't form the words with her thick tongue and she didn't have the breath to utter them anyway. Her vision darkened as unconsciousness—or maybe it was death—threatened.

Chapter Fourteen

Cooper's skin tingled from the swipe of Tanya's hot tongue. His heart pounded in his chest and his body was tense with desire. Then he heard her gasp—faint, as it was. A few moments ago her face had been flushed, her eyes twinkling as she'd teased him.

Now her face was deathly pale and her eyes were rolling back in her head. He reached out, catching her just as she crumpled, her legs giving way beneath her slight weight. Cursing, he swung her up in his arms.

"Mom! Did you put peanuts in the cake?" He remembered other kids hating Tanya because they hadn't been able to have peanut snacks or PB and J sandwiches in school—because of her allergy.

She had been resented and ostracized for her childhood allergy. Just like the asthma, she must not have outgrown it.

"Of course I wouldn't use peanuts," she replied as she rushed over to them. "I know she's allergic."

Her sister and Stephen would know that, too. He peered around the room, searching for Rochelle. She stood next to Nikki, who had been assigned to keep an eye on her. Of course, Logan had backup for their baby sister. He wouldn't have trusted her alone.

"She got peanuts somehow."

His mother swiped a finger over the knife and tasted. "Someone must have put peanut oil in the frosting."

"Do you have an EpiPen?" he asked hopefully. "Did she give you a spare one of those?"

She shook her head. "No, I didn't think she'd need it. I made sure that nothing had peanuts or peanut oil in it."

Someone else had made sure that something had peanut oil in it. Tanya's throat was probably completely closed. He felt the breath leaving her body as it had just a couple of days ago. "Call 911."

"Use this," a female voice said, and Rochelle held out a pen.

Cooper stared at it, trying to determine if this was another trick of hers. A way to finish off her sister right in front of all of them.

"Why do you have it?" he asked, wondering if she'd taken it from Tanya's purse along with the inhaler.

"I have the same allergy," she explained. "I can't have peanuts."

Mrs. Payne grasped her shoulders. "I'm so glad you haven't had a piece of cake."

Yeah, that was convenient. And so was Rochelle offering a pen for the sister she despised. He didn't trust anyone easily, but Rochelle's attitude and actions had given him plenty of reasons to mistrust her.

"Take it!" she yelled at him. "She can't breathe."

"Isn't that what you want?" he asked. "Your sister out of your way?"

She gasped. "I don't want her dead!" She pushed the pen into his hand. "Do you?"

That was the last thing he wanted. If they'd waited for the ambulance for the asthma attack, Tanya would have died. He couldn't wait now either. So he laid her on the floor. And he injected the pen, right through her jeans, into the outside of her thigh. Years ago she had told him how to do it—in case she needed help. And he had never forgotten.

Just as he'd never forgotten anything concerning Tanya Chesterfield.

She gasped again but then she dragged in a deep breath. Her eyes opened and she stared up at all of them. "I'm okay," she assured them.

Sirens blared as first responders pulled up outside the church.

"I don't need to go to the hospital."

"You're going," he insisted as he lifted her again to carry her upstairs to the ambulance. He wasn't entirely convinced that the medication Rochelle offered wouldn't have some horrible side effect. He had to make sure that Tanya would really be okay.

Because he didn't know what he would do if he lost his wife…

"You're lucky you're not really married to me," Tanya told Cooper, whose long, muscular body was awkwardly sprawled in a chair beside her bed. "You've already spent enough time in the hospital with me."

"Too much," he readily agreed.

She blinked against the sting of tears. "I'm sorry. Usually my allergy and my asthma aren't issues…"

"But someone's using your illnesses to try to kill you," he said. "Someone who knows you well."

"It can't be someone from one of my cases, then," she said. She'd really wished it was—some bad person holding a grudge against her would be so much easier to accept.

Cooper sighed. "It actually could be. Or at least that's what Nikki is trying to convince me."

Because Nikki and Rochelle were friends. It was probably harder for Nikki to doubt her friend than it was for Tanya to doubt her sister. Tanya had found it harder to doubt Stephen.

"Nikki informs me that stalkers are very thorough." He leaned back in his chair and reached out an arm to open the door.

"Nik," he called to the auburn-haired woman who then came into the room. She must have been waiting in the hall. And she hadn't been alone. Rochelle walked inside with her. But she hesitated near the door, as if uncertain of her welcome.

Since Cooper was glaring at her, she had reason to feel unwelcome. But at least this time she had come to check on Tanya.

Last time, she hadn't seemed to care that her sister had nearly died. That was why Tanya had found it so easy to doubt her...because she had never understood her.

"You're really all right?" Nikki anxiously asked.

Tanya nodded. "I'm more embarrassed that this keeps happening." It made her feel like a child again—that demons she hadn't fought since childhood had come back to haunt her and had nearly made her a ghost, as well.

"It's not your fault," Nikki said. "Someone's after you. I told Cooper that it could be the stalker."

"That's why I called you in here," he said. "To explain your theory to Tanya." He stood up. "I need to check in with Parker and Logan." He stared at his sister. "You got this?"

Nikki apparently knew he was talking about more than the theory. He was talking about keeping Tanya safe from Rochelle. She nodded her assurance.

He stepped into the hall without even a glance back

at Tanya. Was he sick of her? Sick of all the drama she'd brought to his life?

"I don't understand how someone could know so much about me," she said. Unless that person had been close to her, had grown up with her.

"Stalkers are relentless," Nikki said. "I've studied them in my psych and criminology classes. A stalker will usually go through their obsession's trash. Some savvy ones hack into their obsession's email."

She shuddered at the thought of someone invading her privacy—reading her private correspondence, seeing what she ate, drank and used and then discarded.

"You'd rather think it's me than a stalker?" Rochelle finally spoke—with her usual hostility.

"Of course not," Tanya said, but she felt a twinge of guilt. "Giving Cooper that EpiPen, you saved me."

"I had to force that pen on Cooper," Rochelle said. "He thinks I want you dead."

Tanya was sick of not knowing who wanted her dead. So she asked, "Don't you?"

Rochelle cursed and shook her head. "You really hate me."

"No," Tanya said. "You're the one who hates me. And I don't know why. What did I do?"

"It's more like what you didn't do," Rochelle replied.

"I don't understand."

"No. And you never bothered to try. You were just like Mom," Rochelle accused her.

"What do you mean?"

"She was obsessed with Dad no matter how big a louse he was. And you were obsessed with a boy."

"What are you talking about?"

"Cooper Payne. You were obsessed with him then. You're obsessed with him now. I saw how you were looking at him back at the *party*. You wanted to eat him instead of the cake."

She couldn't deny that, and heat rushed to her face with embarrassment.

"She would have been safer if she had," Nikki remarked. "Jeez, Rochelle, someone's trying to kill her. Someone's trying to kill your sister. Can't you get over her not paying enough attention to you when you were young?"

"You were so much younger," Tanya reminded her.

Rochelle crossed her arms over her chest and stubbornly held on to her resentment. "Not that much."

"Six years."

"It is a lot," Nikki said. "My brothers still treat me like a little kid."

"I'm sorry," Tanya said. "I should have made more time for you." She should have made her sister feel important since their mother never had; Andrea Chesterfield was nothing like Penny Payne, who had always put her children first, even over her own grief.

Rochelle shook her head and blinked hard as if fighting back tears. "It's just not fair, you know…"

"What's not?"

"You're so beautiful." Rochelle said it with such bitterness it sounded more like a condemnation than a compliment. "You get all the guys."

She only wanted one. "That's not true."

"You had Stephen." Her breath caught as if she was about the cry. "And now you have Cooper. He's the one you really want. What did you do to Stephen to get him out of your way?"

Tanya gasped in shock now. "You think I would hurt Stephen?"

"Absolutely," Rochelle said, "because you've never felt

about him like you do about Cooper Payne. You probably agreed to marry him to get the money because your birthday was coming up and Cooper wasn't back. But then when he got back, Stephen conveniently—*for you*—went missing."

Her sister was in love with Stephen. It was so obvious to her now—because of how she loved Cooper.

"Are you drunk?" Nikki asked her friend.

"No!" Rochelle snapped at her.

"Were you drunk when you sent Stephen that email?" Tanya asked.

Embarrassment flooded Rochelle's face, turning her skin a bright pink. "Which email?"

She had obviously sent him more than one.

Nikki grimaced. She must not have told her friend that her brothers or probably she, since she was the computer expert, had found those emails. And Tanya probably wasn't supposed to share that information. But she didn't care. She wanted answers.

"I'm talking about the email where you beg him to dump me and marry you and you'll give him all your inheritance," she replied.

Tears shimmered in Rochelle's eyes. "It didn't work. You took Stephen for granted all these years, but he stayed loyal to you. He stayed true to you." She blinked back the tears, and anger hardened her gaze. "Too bad you can't stay the same."

"Wh-what do you mean?" Tanya stammered as embarrassment rushed over her now, her face heating with it.

"It's obvious you're sleeping with Cooper," Rochelle replied.

And Nikki gasped. She knew the marriage was only supposed to be one of convenience.

But Tanya's feelings for her reluctant stand-in groom were anything but convenient.

"So I can't give Stephen all the money anymore," Rochelle continued. "You've consummated your marriage before your birthday, so you'll be able to claim your half of Grandfather's money now. Hell, you'll probably wind up with all of it."

Because Stephen was the man Rochelle had wanted to marry, and he was gone.

"You really don't know where he is?" she asked.

"Cooper just stepped into the hall," Rochelle replied. "Can't you stand being away from him for more than a couple of minutes?"

Truthfully, she couldn't. She missed him already. She'd gotten so used to him sticking close to her. But that was because he was her bodyguard—not because he was her loving husband.

"I'm talking about Stephen," she clarified. "Where is he?"

"Why do you think I would know?"

Tanya opened her mouth to reply, but Nikki interrupted, "You've obviously been in contact with him."

"Not since he disappeared," Rochelle said. "I sent him those emails before that."

"That last one was the night he disappeared," Nikki pointed out.

"*You* were the one who found the emails!" Rochelle realized. "And instead of coming to me with them, you went to *her?* I thought you were *my* friend."

Nikki sighed. "Of course I am. I told my brothers."

"*Why?*"

"Because I'm working a case," Nikki unapologetically explained. "Someone's been trying to kill your sister."

"And you all think it's me?" Rochelle looked ready

to burst into tears. But instead she burst out of the room and nearly ran down Cooper in the process.

"You missed all the fun," Nikki accused him.

"What happened?"

"What usually happens when I try to talk to my sister," Tanya replied. "She winds up hating me more." But did she hate her enough to try to kill her?

"You're so lucky you have a fabulous sister like me," Nikki said as she slid her arm around her brother's waist.

Cooper leaned down and kissed her forehead. "I am very lucky."

Tanya envied their relationship. Even though Cooper had been gone for years, he had remained close to his family. Maybe she and Rochelle needed more distance. As offended as Rochelle was, Tanya doubted she would be seeing her again anytime soon.

Tanya found it hard to believe Rochelle had anything to do with the attempts on her life. "I gave Rochelle a reason to hate me this time," she admitted, "when I accused her of trying to kill me."

"You accused her?"

"Not in so many words," Nikki said. "But she picked up on the suspicion—your suspicion."

He nodded. "I am suspicious of her."

"I'm not," Tanya said. "Not anymore anyways. She was too hurt." She had hurt her sister for no reason.

"Sometimes the best defense is a strong offense," Cooper said.

Nikki elbowed him. "You're always so suspicious."

"You need to be, too, if you're going to watch Tanya for me while I check something out."

Pride stinging, Tanya replied, "I am about to turn thirty years old. I don't need a babysitter."

"No," Cooper agreed. "You need a bodyguard."

Tanya wished she could claim that she could defend herself, but if he gave her another gun, she would probably shoot off her own foot.

"You're letting me work as a bodyguard?" Nikki asked, her eyes wide with surprise and hope.

Cooper glanced away from his sister. "I would, kid. I would. But Logan insists that Candace—"

"That jerk," Nikki cursed her oldest brother. "Is he in the hall?"

Cooper nodded slowly—almost reluctantly.

Nikki pushed past him to run out of the room.

"Lot of people running out of here today," he remarked with a wry grin.

"Yes," Tanya agreed with a pointed stare.

"Hey, I need to check this out," he said.

"The doctor's releasing me. I just have to wait for his final orders," she reminded him. "Then I can go with you."

"Absolutely not," he said.

"I'm sure your brothers can handle it." And some sick feeling in the pit of her stomach had her wishing that he would let them because she was afraid that something was going to happen to him. "*You* don't have to go."

"Parker and Logan will be there, too," he assured her, "but *I* still need to go."

"Where?" she asked as her own suspicions overwhelmed her. "What are you so determined to check out?"

"Parker got a lead from one of his informants."

"To Stephen's whereabouts?"

He nodded.

"Are you sure it's a real lead?"

"Not yet."

"But what if it's not?" she asked as that sick feeling grew in intensity. "What if it's a trap?"

"That's why you can't go along. I want you safe."

"I want you safe, too," she said. She just wanted him...

He must have seen the longing in her face because he stepped closer to the bed. "I told you before—this is what I do, what I've been doing, what I'm always going to do."

Maybe it was good that their marriage wasn't real then because she wasn't certain she could handle worrying about him every day when he left for work. But her job wasn't exactly safe either. As Nikki had pointed out, the person after her could have been someone who'd felt she'd wronged them as their caseworker.

"I know," she said. "But I'm worried..."

He leaned down and maybe he'd intended to kiss her forehead, but she lifted her face so that his mouth met hers. And she kissed him with all the need burning inside her.

He pulled back, panting for breath, his pupils dilated with passion. "Tanya..."

That sick feeling persisted, warning her that something horrible could happen to him. Like maybe this time the shooter wouldn't miss.

"Please don't go..."

He kissed her again, just a quick brushing of his lips across hers. She tried to cling, but he pulled back and assured her, "I'll be fine."

She watched him walk away, worrying that this might be the last time. That she might lose him again. Forever...

COOPER USUALLY LISTENED to his gut, but he didn't let the warning twisting his stomach into knots stop him from moving toward the warehouse. It was probably just

Tanya's nerves that he'd picked up on. Or it was his nerves over leaving her alone.

Sure, she wasn't exactly alone. She had Nikki protecting her and Candace protecting both of them. Nikki was green. But Candace had already saved Logan earlier that day; she was an experienced, expert bodyguard.

Tanya was safe. He wasn't so sure about him and his brothers. All the lights were burned out in the parking lot of the warehouse. The building had been abandoned a long time. The metal siding was more rust than whatever color it might have been at one time. And boards covered the windows.

If Stephen had been brought here, Cooper hoped he hadn't been hurt. The place sure as hell didn't look very sanitary or safe.

"You see anything?" the whisper emanated from his cell phone.

Parker was covering the front of the building while Cooper sneaked around a side to the loading docks in the back. With only the flashlight attached to the barrel of his gun to guide him, Cooper found steps leading up to the docks. Like the building, the metal stairs were rusted and protested his weight with creaks and screeches as he climbed them.

"Nothing yet," he whispered back. He shone his light below the docks and noticed that a ramp had been pushed up to the garage door on the end. He headed across the concrete, which seemed to crumble beneath his feet, to that last door.

"Nothing over here," Logan reported from the other side of the building. "Not even a door…" The phone rustled and the other man cursed. He'd gotten to the side of the building that had been overgrown with weeds and thorny shrubs.

Cooper had passed a few doors, rusted ones with equally rusted locks holding them down. Except for the last one. A smashed lock lay on the ground below, next to the rusted ramp, and the door was so rusted that although it had gone up, it hadn't gone all the way back down.

"I found a way in," he reported.

"Wait for us," Logan advised.

But Cooper had already shone his light beneath the door. It glinted off something shiny and black. He crouched down to crawl beneath the door. The rusted metal caught at the back of his jacket, holding him up until he tugged free with a rip of leather.

"What was that?" Parker asked. He'd heard the tear of fabric.

"Nothing." But he'd found more than nothing. He had found a familiar black vehicle. The back tires were both flat. It was *the* black vehicle—the one that had nearly run down Tanya. "But the car..."

"The car?" Logan asked. "I'm on my way around the side. Stay put."

But Cooper focused on the trunk. What if...

What if Stephen had really been abducted?

He glanced around the warehouse, the beam of his flashlight bouncing off old crates, before turning his attention back to the trunk. He grabbed a small tool kit from his pocket and slid a pick into the lock. A couple twists and pulls and the lock clicked. The lid popped up.

He drew in a deep breath before lifting the lid the rest of the way. The trunk was empty. No body. But when he flashed his light inside, the beam illuminated a dark stain. He reached inside the trunk and touched the carpet. The stain was sticky yet...

He lifted his hand and shone the beam onto his skin. The smear was dark red: blood.

Stephen's? Had Cooper been wrong to doubt him? Was he alive? Or had his body been dumped?

He shuddered with regret.

With a rumble that shook the entire warehouse, an engine started. It wasn't the car's, but the car began to move. Cooper slammed down the trunk lid and squinted as bright lights from a forklift blinded him. It was pushing against the front bumper and lifting the car up— driving it into him. He stumbled back as he lifted his gun and fired at the forklift.

But then there was nothing beneath his feet as the edge of the concrete dock crumbled and gave way. He dropped to the ground below and hit the asphalt with such force that all the breath left his body.

But the forklift kept coming, pushing the car ahead of it. He stared up at the undercarriage of the big black sedan as it fell—on top of him.

Chapter Fifteen

Fear clutched Tanya's heart so fiercely that she was physically in pain. She gasped from the force of it.

"Are you all right?" Nikki asked.

She shook her head. "Not until we know if they're okay."

Candace paced across the kitchen of the safe house where she and Nikki had brought Tanya. This particular safe *house* was Candace's own apartment. And it wasn't in the safest area of town, but then she doubted anyone would dare mess with the female bodyguard.

She must have worn a wig to pass herself off as Tanya because her hair was short and brown. And she was taller and more muscular.

Nobody would mess with Candace. Tanya felt safe with her; it was Cooper she was worried about. "Have you heard anything?" she asked the woman.

Candace shook her head as she lowered the cell phone. "Logan's not picking up." Her facial muscles were tense with concern. "He always picks up…"

Nikki's head jerked in a sharp nod. "He always does…"

"Even when he's being shot at," Tanya remembered Cooper's call to his oldest brother.

"I should have gone with him," Candace said.

Nikki patted the bodyguard's shoulder. "I'm sure he's fine. I'm sure they're all fine."

Candace gripped the cell phone tightly, as if she were somehow reaching out to Logan through it.

Tanya didn't even know Cooper's cell-phone number, and he was her husband.

Was?

Had she already lost him as that gut-wrenching premonition had warned her?

"Logan shouldn't have gone out right now," Candace said. "He shouldn't have risked it…"

Tanya was confused. "Cooper's the one the shooter is after. He just mistook Logan for Cooper." Which was a mistake that Stephen wouldn't have made; he knew the Payne family as well as she did.

"I'm not so sure about that," Candace admitted.

Of course. Logan might have made enemies of his own—while he was a detective with River City Police Department or even through Payne Protection.

"What are you saying?" Nikki asked, her usually smooth brow furrowed with concern.

"He didn't tell you?" Candace asked with a flash of surprise.

"Tell me what?" Nikki asked. "Has *he* been getting threats?"

"Just the usual ones."

Nikki sighed.

And Tanya grasped that apparently she wasn't the only one with a stalker. "What ones?"

"From the daughter of the man who shot his father," Candace explained. "She's furious that Logan keeps showing up to every parole hearing."

Tanya nodded in understanding. "Cooper told me that Logan is determined to keep Mr. Payne's killer in prison."

"He succeeded," Candace shared. "The man died a couple of days ago."

Nikki cursed.

"He didn't tell you," Candace answered her own question. Her lips curved into a slight smile as if she was pleased that her boss had confided in her.

Tanya wondered if he'd told Cooper, because if he had, her husband hadn't shared that news with her. Of course, he'd been a little preoccupied trying to keep her alive—and making love with her.

Nikki grabbed her own cell phone and punched the screen. "Damn it! Answer!"

"I just tried Logan," Candace reminded her.

"I'm trying Parker."

"He's not picking up either?"

Nikki punched her screen again and then cursed again. "Neither is Cooper."

Tanya's knees weakened as fear overwhelmed her.

Candace blinked quickly as if fighting tears. She obviously felt more than employee devotion for her boss; she was in love with him. And Nikki was so scared her eyes were wide and dark in her pale face.

Tanya wanted to offer them comfort. But she needed comfort herself. She needed Cooper, his strong arms wrapped around her—keeping her safe as he had the past few days. She needed her husband.

"Are you okay?" Nikki asked. "You don't look so good."

"I'm tired," she said.

Candace gestured down the hall. "Make use of the guest room I showed you earlier. The bed is comfortable."

Tanya wasn't likely to succumb to sleep—not when she was shaking with nerves. She just needed to be alone, to shed the tears stinging her eyes. She couldn't cry in front of the other women—not when they were both trying so hard to be strong.

She went down the hall, located the guest room then closed the door behind her but didn't turn on the light. She fumbled around in the dark until she found the bed. She dropped onto it and curled into a ball, wrapping her arms around herself—holding herself together since Cooper wasn't there.

She shouldn't have let him go. She was his wife now. Wasn't he supposed to listen to her? Wasn't that how marriage worked? But their marriage wasn't real—even though they'd consummated it. It wasn't real because Cooper didn't love her the way she loved him.

Why hadn't she buried her pride and told him? Maybe if she had, he wouldn't have left her.

But he was Cooper Payne. He didn't fear anything. He never had or he wouldn't have joined the Marines after high school graduation. And he was right; he could take care of himself. And his brothers, as he had taken care of her.

He had to be okay…

She squeezed her eyes shut, but tears leaked out of the corners and streaked down the sides of her face into the pillow beneath her head. Maybe she had fallen asleep, because she awoke disoriented, unsure of what had startled her.

Then she heard the noise. A rattling. She glanced to the door. But the knob wasn't moving. She turned toward the window and found that she was too late. It was already open and a dark figure was sliding over the sill. She opened her mouth to scream, but a big hand closed over her mouth.

Had the person killed Cooper to get him out of the

way? And now he intended to kill her? She couldn't count on Cooper to save her. She had to save herself.

She struggled in his arms, thrashing around so that her elbow jammed into his aching ribs and her knee nearly struck a more sensitive part of his body. Pain overwhelmed him, and he cursed. Then he shushed her. "It's okay. It's me."

She tensed so abruptly that he worried he'd hurt her. He'd wrapped his arms tightly around her while clamping one hand to her mouth. He didn't want the others to know he was in the room with her.

He was supposed to be in the hospital, but he'd checked himself out against doctor's orders. It wasn't as if he would be any safer in the hospital. Tanya hadn't been; he grimaced as he remembered how the killer had tried to smother her.

Was the kidnapper a killer yet? Was Stephen dead?

He moved his hand from her mouth, his palm ablaze from the contact with her silky-soft lips.

"It's you," she murmured as if unable to believe he was real. "It's really you?"

"I'm glad you didn't shoot me this time," Cooper said with a chuckle. But that chuckle shook his ribs, and he groaned.

"Are you okay?" she asked. "What happened tonight? None of you were answering your phones!"

He suddenly noticed the tears on her face. And concern was in her voice. She'd worried about him.

"I'm fine," he said. But even he shuddered as he remembered how close that car had come to falling on top of him. If he hadn't gathered the strength to roll out of the way, it might have crushed him.

His brothers had been so worried about him that they'd

both let the damn suspect slip away again. Who exactly was after him? And her?

He kept his arms clenched tightly around her, needing to feel her warmth and softness—her heart beating in unison with his—the same frantic rhythm. Like when they'd made love, they were perfectly in sync.

"What happened?" she asked. "Why didn't you answer your phones?"

"We were a little preoccupied."

"Did you find Stephen?"

He grimaced as if she'd elbowed him again. Of course she was worried about Stephen. "No," he said. "But we found the car that nearly ran you over."

"So it was a real lead—not a setup?"

He hesitated. He had never liked hearing "I told you so." But she was entitled to say it. "You were right."

"It was a setup? But the car was there."

"The police have it now." Or what was left of it. "They'll process it for evidence." Especially the bloodstain in the trunk.

"Why was it a setup?"

"There was a forklift…" He shrugged and then grimaced again.

Her eyes must have adjusted to the dark because she saw it and ran her fingers over his face. "You're hurt."

"Just a little bruised." Like all his ribs and his back. "I've been hurt worse before."

She gasped in alarm. "Don't tell me that."

"Why not?"

"I didn't let myself think of you over there—in danger. I didn't let myself think that you might never come back." She shuddered. "But every once in a while the thoughts crept in…like you did through the window." She stared up at him. "Why did you come through the window?"

That had been extreme—especially since he'd had to straddle the ledge between the fire escape and her window. "I don't want the others to know I'm here."

"Why not? Don't they want you here?"

"Not tonight," he admitted.

"Because you're hurt."

"I'm fine." And he was, now that he knew she was safe, now that he was with her. Or maybe the painkillers had just finally kicked in, because he didn't feel it now. He felt too many others things with her soft body pressed against his.

Her fingers lingered on his face, stroking along his cheekbones and then his jaw. "I'm sorry…"

"It's not your fault," he said.

"I'm sorry about your father."

"That happened years ago," he reminded her. But sometimes it felt like just days or hours—the pain and loss would hit him so hard. Leaving home hadn't lessened that pain as he'd thought it would.

"But your father's killer just died," she said, "and that must bring that all back."

He tensed in shock. "What?"

"Didn't Logan tell you either? Nikki didn't know."

He suspected Parker didn't know either. Damn Logan. Damn him for trying so hard to take their father's place as the patriarch and the protector.

"Candace thinks that the man's daughter might have been the one who shot at Logan earlier today."

"When he was posing as me?" He shrugged. "I don't know…"

"You don't think so? Whatever happened with the forklift—could it have been meant for Logan?" she asked.

He sighed. "No. It was definitely meant for me. And

it involved the car that nearly killed you. What happened in that warehouse had nothing to do with Logan."

"And everything to do with me…" Her voice cracked with emotion. Guilt?

"It's not your fault."

"I just want it to be over…"

The attacks or their marriage? When one ended, so would the other. Cooper had to keep that in mind so he didn't think it was real. So he didn't think she was actually his wife.

He eased his arms from around her and dropped them back to his sides. "I should let you sleep…"

"I can't," she said. "Not without you…" She wrapped her arms around him and tugged him down beside her.

He felt a twinge, but the painkillers must have kicked in because it wasn't that bad. Or maybe her holding him just felt so good…

"Tanya…"

"I was so worried about you," she said. Her lips touched his cheek, then slid across until she found his mouth. She pressed whisper-soft kisses to his lips, as if afraid that she might hurt him.

He gripped the back of her head, tangling his fingers in her hair, and pulled her closer. Then he deepened the kiss, pressing his lips tightly to hers.

She gasped against his mouth, and he took advantage of her open lips, sliding his tongue between them. In and out. He tasted her—the sweetness that was only Tanya. Her arms tightened around him.

But he pulled back. Not because he was in pain but because he was overdressed. He quickly stripped off his clothes, careful this time to keep the gun within reach of the bed. While he stripped, she'd done the same—tossing aside her shirt and pants and those little strips of lace and satin that had driven him nearly out of his mind.

But he preferred this—skin sliding over skin—as he joined her on the bed again. Her thigh slid between his, her hip rubbing against his erection. It throbbed with arousal. He had never wanted anyone the way he wanted—the way he *needed*—his *wife*.

If the way she was touching him, kissing him, was any indication, she wanted him, too. Or she'd been really worried about him.

If that was the case, he loved the way she expressed her relief. Her lips closed around him, taking him into her mouth, while her fingers teased his nipples. He groaned.

"Am I hurting you?" she asked, all concern.

"You're killing me," he said. "But in a good way."

"Let me make it all better," she offered.

But he stopped her, tangling his hand in her hair again, before she could lower her head back down. He kissed her passionately—their tongues swirling, and their breath coming in quick pants.

Just her kiss nearly had him at his breaking point. He felt as if he was going to burst. He wanted her as crazy for him as he was for her, so he teased her nipples with his fingers, tugging gently at them.

She moaned into his mouth. Then he moved one hand lower, between her legs. And now she whimpered and squirmed against him. Then she bit her lip, holding in a scream while she came—her body shuddering against his.

He shuddered, too, with need. She pushed him back on the bed, and he didn't even feel the pain of his bruised back. He felt only her as she guided him inside her. She rode him, sliding up and down, rocking back and forth. She drove him out of his mind.

She shuddered again as she reached her peak. Instead of biting her lip this time, she bit his. And he welcomed the bite.

It snapped the last of his control, and he joined her in the madness, his body jerking as he thrust deep and filled her. She dropped onto his chest, her heart beating frantically—her breath a hot pant against his throat. Their bodies were still joined, so he didn't move her. He just wrapped his arms around her and held her close.

The pain pills must have really kicked in because he felt sleep coming. And he couldn't fight it off as he had so many times before. The others were in the apartment; if someone else sneaked through her window and she screamed, they would help her. She was safe. So he slept...

SHE HATED TO leave him. But it was only for a moment to answer the call of nature. Carefully, so she wouldn't wake him, Tanya slid out from his embrace and rose from the bed. Immediately she felt empty and cold.

She reached for the robe Candace had left on the back of the bedroom door and wrapped it around herself. Then she slipped quietly out of the room and into the hall.

"Is he in there?" Candace asked.

Tanya jumped and clutched a hand to her throat at the surprise of finding the female bodyguard waiting in the hall. "What?"

"Logan called," she uttered those words with great relief, "and said that Cooper checked himself out against doctor's orders."

Her hand trembled. "How badly is he hurt?"

"Bruised ribs. He hit the asphalt hard when the forklift nearly pushed that car on top of him."

Tanya shuddered.

"The doctor said the fall alone could have broken his back. They wanted to keep him overnight for observation."

The darkness in her room and now in the hall had already grown thinner as night slipped away. Daylight would break soon. So maybe he hadn't left too soon.

"Logan figured he'd broken out to come here," Candace continued, "to come to you."

Tanya nodded. "He's here. He came through the window."

The other woman shook her head. "The fire escape is a couple of windows over. He must have edged along the window ledges."

"Tell Logan he's okay," Tanya said. "Really. He's sleeping now."

"I'll tell him," Candace said as she rushed down the hall—probably to wherever she'd left her cell phone.

Tanya made quick use of the bathroom and returned to the bed where Cooper slept. His breathing was too irregular, as if dreams—or more likely, nightmares—disrupted him. She slipped off the robe and crawled back into bed with him. He had turned toward the wall, so she wrapped her arms around his side and pressed herself to his back.

He grunted and jerked, as if in pain. So she pulled away, giving him room. And giving herself enough room to study his body in the gathering light of dawn.

His back was blue and purple in some spots, dark red in others where the skin was raw. And the usually defined and sculpted muscles were swollen. She understood the doctor's concern now, his reasons for wanting to keep him overnight.

Cooper should have stayed in the hospital. Instead, he'd come to her. Why? It was all her fault.

The car that had nearly crushed him had almost run

her over. That wasn't an accident or coincidence. The killer was sending her a message—that Cooper would meet the same gruesome fate she would.

She shouldn't have married him. If anyone was holding Stephen for ransom, they would have asked for it before now. She didn't need the money. She needed Cooper.

But she couldn't have both.

She really couldn't have either—not without risking Cooper's life. He had been risking his life for years, but that was his choice. She didn't want him risking it for her.

She pressed a gentle kiss to his shoulder. He shifted against the mattress and murmured as if even that soft brush of her lips hurt him. But he didn't awaken. Maybe they had given him pain medication at the hospital that had finally gotten him to sleep.

Or knocked him out.

She was counting on the latter. She edged farther away from him and then rolled off the side of the mattress. The light of dawn wasn't bright enough yet for her to find her clothes without feeling around in the dark. So she felt around on the floor, and her fingers fumbled over something cold and hard. Revulsion had her stomach pitching over finding the gun.

She had nearly shot Cooper. Fortunately, she hadn't known how to aim the thing. She kept her hand on the weapon and considered taking it. But with what she was about to do, hopefully she wouldn't need it anymore.

If the money was what had put her in danger, she didn't want it. She wanted nothing to do with it. Or with Cooper's gun.

Until everyone learned what she'd done, he might need it to protect himself. She passed over the gun and grabbed up her clothes. As quickly and quietly as she could, she dressed.

Cooper was going to be angry over what she was about to do. But she would rather go out alone and risk her life than put him in danger again.

She leaned back over the bed, but this time she pressed her lips to his cheek. He was out, so he probably would not hear her. But she needed to tell him what she'd been too cowardly to declare when he was awake. She needed to know that she had at last said the words. So she whispered them into his ear.

"I love you."

She waited to see if he murmured anything back—not that she expected him to return her feelings. He'd pointed out over and over again that he was only doing his job. She wasn't paying him, but she was definitely going to fire him.

She glanced to the door but remembered how Candace had appeared in the hall the minute Tanya had stepped out of the room. She couldn't go out the door.

So she would have to go out the way Cooper had come in—through the window. He'd left it unlatched, so all she had to do was press her hands against the glass and push up the sash. Cool air blew through the opening, lifting the rumpled sheet that barely covered Cooper's naked body.

She held her breath, afraid that he would wake up and stop her. But he didn't move—not even to cover himself. Was he really all right? He'd left the hospital against doctor's orders. Maybe she shouldn't leave him…

But then her leaving him was exactly what she needed to do in order to keep him safe. She lifted one leg over the windowsill, but her foot met only empty space. Candace had said there was a ledge. She drew her foot closer to the brick wall of the apartment building, and she found it—six or so skinny inches of concrete. She turned her foot sideways and set it firmly on the ledge before crawling out through the window.

She clutched at the brick wall as dizziness overwhelmed her. She shouldn't have looked down—because now she could look nowhere else. Her knees trembled and her heart raced.

The apartment was on the third floor of the building. Until then—staring down into the abyss of the alley—Tanya hadn't realized how far up three stories was. Nor had she considered how far she would fall if she slipped.

Hitting the asphalt from the height of a loading dock could have broken Cooper's back. Hitting it from this height would probably break every bone in her body.

Already bruised and wounded, Cooper had sidled across this ledge to get to her. Why? Only to protect her?

Just how seriously did the man take his job?

Too seriously—when it was likely to get him killed. She had to do this, had to save him from saving her. Because she didn't want to wake him with the cool breeze, she maneuvered around on the ledge enough to push down the window. She couldn't lower it completely—not without bending all the way over, and if she did that, she would fall for certain. But crouching down strained the muscles in her already shaking legs and her feet began to slip.

Clutching at the wall again, she regained her tenuous position on the ledge. And inch by inch she sidled across it toward the fire escape. It was exactly three dark windows over—probably twelve feet. But to Tanya, who was freezing with cold and fright, it may as well have been a mile. She panted and shook as if she'd run twenty.

Her hands were cold and nearly numb from scraping across the brick wall when she reached out for the railing of the fire escape. Her fingers slipped, knocking her off balance so much that her foot began to slide off the ledge.

Had she made it all those feet only to fall now—when she was so close to the fire escape? The killer would be thrilled—he wouldn't have to try to shoot her or poison her anymore. Tanya was going to kill herself with her probably misguided attempt to save the man she loved.

Chapter Sixteen

Cooper hated sleeping because usually his dreams haunted him with memories of things he had seen or done, things that he was almost able to forget when he was awake. But now he awakened with a smile and a good memory.

Of making love with Tanya.

And of her saying, "I love you."

He must have dreamed that—must have imagined her whispering those words into his ear. Until a few days ago, she had been engaged to marry another man. It didn't matter that Cooper was the one she had actually wed; he was only a substitute for the man she really loved.

The smile slid away from his face, and he forced open eyes that felt gritty with sleep and probably the aftereffects of the painkillers.

The meds had worn off, because his back ached like hell. And his ribs protested every breath he drew into his lungs. And he sucked in a deep breath as he scanned the empty room.

She was gone. Had someone grabbed her while he slept? The window was open a few inches—more than he'd left it when he'd come inside that way. And the gun was still inside its holster next to the bed. He reached for it.

If someone had broken in while he slept, wouldn't she have used it just as she'd tried using it the night she'd almost shot him? Tanya was tough; she wouldn't have survived all the attempts on her life if she wasn't.

Maybe she had opened the window for air. Or because he'd gotten too hot sharing the only full-size bed with her. He wasn't hot now, with the cool wind blowing over his bare skin. He hurriedly dressed, ignoring the twinges in his back and ribs, as he pulled on the clothes he'd discarded so quickly the night before.

Her clothes were gone—just as she was. But with the sun only just streaking between the buildings and shining across that open windowsill, it was early yet. Not much past dawn.

He hadn't given her much choice last night before jumping into bed with her. But she had seemed willing then. His skin flushed with heat and desire as he remembered how thoroughly she had made love to him. She had definitely been willing.

So where was she? He opened the door and stepped into the hall. Voices drew him toward the kitchen, where he hoped to find her with the others, sitting around the small round table or leaning against the cabinets. Nikki sat at the table staring at the screen of the laptop in front of her, while Parker leaned back, the chair on two legs, against the wall, with his cell phone pressed to his ear.

Logan reclined against the cabinets, his arms crossed over his chest, like a teacher surveying his class. As the oldest, he'd always thought he knew more than the rest of them. But that was probably just because he kept what he knew secret—like the death of their father's killer.

Cooper would deal with that later, though. He was more concerned with who wasn't in the kitchen than who was. Candace was missing, which was odd since this was her place. But she could have been in the bathroom or her bedroom.

Tanya was gone. And he knew it because of how empty and alone he felt even with his family present. They glanced at him in the doorway, but there was no surprise on their faces. They'd known where he'd gone after checking himself out of the hospital.

What about Tanya? "Where is she?"

And a better question, why were they all there when the person they were supposed to be protecting wasn't? What kind of bodyguards were Payne Protection?

"Did somebody—" his voice cracked with emotion "—take her?" While he'd slept peacefully in the same bed with her? What the hell kind of bodyguard was he?

"Nobody grabbed her," Logan assured him. "Candace saw her leave of her own accord."

"Maybe she got sick of everybody babysitting her," Nikki suggested. "I know how frustrating it is when nobody trusts you to take care of yourself."

"You didn't see her leave," Logan pointed out. "You're not ready to be a bodyguard on your own yet."

Cooper couldn't defend her any more than he could defend himself for having let Tanya slip away.

"She didn't come out of the door," Nikki said in an attempt to defend herself. "She went out the window."

He cursed under his breath since he'd given her the idea. And because he could envision her precariously balancing on that narrow ledge. "She could have fallen..."

And that fall would have killed her. His heart lurched with pain and loss. Was that why they were all here and not out protecting her? Because she was really gone?

"She didn't fall," Logan assured him.

The pain in his chest eased slightly. She wasn't dead. She was just gone.

"You could have fallen, too, when you sneaked in that way," Nikki said, her eyes wide with fear. "You could have fallen *again*." Obviously their brothers had filled her in on what had happened at the warehouse.

"I'm fine," he said.

"You should let the doctor determine that," Nikki said. "You should go back to the hospital."

"Hell, no," he replied. "The only place I'm going is to find Tanya—which all of you should be doing instead of standing around *here*."

"Candace is following her," Logan explained. "She'll make sure Tanya stays safe."

He wasn't so sure about that. "She's not as good as you think she is. She let me slip into Tanya's room—"

"She knew it was you," Logan replied. "I warned her you were coming when I'd discovered you'd snuck out of the hospital."

"But she let Tanya sneak out..." So had he. His gut churned with guilt over having fallen asleep when he should have been protecting her.

Logan nodded. "She saw her on the ledge, but she didn't dare risk startling her and causing her to fall."

It was a risk she'd been wise not to take. But Cooper suspected there'd been another reason—like her boss's orders. "You wanted to see where she'd go, didn't you?"

Logan nodded again.

"You can't suspect her of being involved in this," he said.

"Why not?"

"Because she's nearly been killed time and again."

"Nearly," Logan pointed out.

"You suspect Rochelle," Nikki reminded him with a trace of resentment. "And even Stephen..."

A pang of guilt struck him. The blood he'd found in

the trunk of that car proved a body had been moved in it. Stephen's? He may have even been inside it when Cooper had fired those shots at the car to stop it from running down Tanya.

"Not Tanya," he insisted. "She has no motive…"

"She has the same motive everyone else has," Logan said. "The money…"

He shook his head. "She couldn't have acted alone. She wasn't driving the car that chased her down. She wasn't firing the shots into her apartment."

Logan nodded. "She didn't act alone."

"That's why you let her go, to see not only where she'd go but who she would meet."

Logan nodded again.

"It's not Stephen," he said. "They would have just gotten married…"

"But maybe he got cold feet," Nikki said.

Over marrying Tanya? Cooper doubted it.

"And she got mad at him," Nikki continued.

Mad enough to hurt him? He doubted that even more. "You're wrong about this."

"Probably," Logan agreed.

"Where is she?" By now his brother, who thought he knew everything, probably knew.

"She took a cab to her grandfather's house."

She'd hated that place nearly as much as Cooper had. "Why?"

"It's hers now," Nikki reminded him.

He shook his head. "It doesn't matter to her. That house—the money…"

"Then why did she marry you?" Logan asked.

"In case there was a ransom demand made for Stephen," he reminded them. "This was all about Stephen." It hurt remembering that the woman he loved—the woman he'd married—was in love with another man.

"There was no ransom demand," Nikki said quietly, as if she knew how badly he was already hurting.

His head throbbed along with his back, pain pounding at his temples, as he tried to process what his family was telling him. To doubt Tanya? And now he knew how she'd felt when he'd tried to make her do the same with Stephen. He knew exactly how she'd felt because he loved her.

"How long have you been thinking this?" he asked Logan. He wasn't above lashing out at him when he was in pain. He'd done it when their dad had died. "And keeping it to yourself—like you keep everything!"

Parker clicked off his cell phone and slid it into his pocket. "What are you talking about? What's he keeping to himself?"

Cooper turned on his other brother. "You know that Dad's killer died in prison."

Parker shrugged as if it didn't matter to him, and it didn't matter to any of them as much as it did to Logan. "Not because he told me."

"Candace just told me," Nikki chimed in.

That must have been how Tanya had learned about it. He asked his brothers, "Why didn't either of you tell me?"

"You've been a little preoccupied getting married and all," Logan reminded him. "And truthfully, I didn't know if it would matter to any of you."

Like it mattered to him. They had all been content with the man being sent to prison. Logan was the one who hadn't been able to let go of his anger. Maybe he could now...

Cooper shrugged off the slight much easier than he

could shrug off his brother's doubts about the woman he loved.

"Doesn't anyone want to know why I was on the phone?" Parker asked. With a grin he announced, "We got a real lead this time."

"You thought that last one was a real lead," Cooper reminded him, flinching as his ribs ached.

"We found the car," Parker reminded him.

He'd nearly wound up with it on top of him, but they had found it. "Have the crime scene techs processed it yet? Have they found any prints?"

Logan nodded. "The blood in the trunk matches the blood from the church—same type, at least. DNA is still backlogged."

"What about prints?"

"The steering wheel was wiped clean on the car and the forklift, too," Logan replied. "Stephen's never been fingerprinted, so we don't know if the ones inside the trunk lid are his."

Someone had been alive inside that trunk—had been banging and trying to get out. Cooper's stomach tightened with dread. "We gotta find him."

"We may have," Parker reminded him. "One of my informants spotted that car at another warehouse before it wound up where we found it."

Another warehouse. Cooper's ribs throbbed as if in protest and he groaned.

"You stay here with Nikki," Logan ordered.

"Of course I don't get to go," Nikki resentfully grumbled.

Logan ignored her and continued, "Parker and I will check it out alone—like we should have last time."

Cooper shook his head. "I'm going, too."

"You're already hurt. Want to finish yourself off?" his oldest brother challenged him.

"I want to finish this," he said. "I want to nail the bastard who's responsible for all the shooting and stuff."

"What if that bastard's Tanya?" Logan asked.

God, the man was more paranoid than Cooper was. "It's not." And he had a feeling it wasn't Stephen either—that he had misjudged his friend. He just hoped he had a chance to make it up to him. "Let's stop wasting time and follow up this lead."

He just hoped it didn't lead them to a body.

TANYA SHIVERED WITH cold and dread. The house—or mausoleum as Cooper had called it—had been closed up for years. So it was freezing inside, with no heat or electricity, and it was musty smelling—exactly like a mausoleum.

Her lungs strained for breath, and she wished she'd thought to bring along her purse with the newly prescribed inhaler inside. But the extra weight of her bag might have been enough to make her lose her balance off the ledge entirely.

She'd barely caught the fire escape in time as it was. Her palms still stung from how hard she'd gripped the cold and rusted metal. She'd had to hang on tightly while she'd swung herself over the railing. Her legs had been shaking so badly it was a wonder she'd made it down all the steps to the alley below.

Her legs still shook a little now. But all the furniture was covered with heavy plastic, leaving her no place to sit down. The floor was hard marble and probably like ice now; she couldn't sit on it either. Only faint light filtered through the thick drapes pulled across the windows. It was so cold and dark and creepy.

It was truly like a mausoleum, just minus the wall of drawers containing urns of ashes. Her grandfather's urn was here, though, sitting on the mantel with a fine coating of dust covering the brass. Was he really in there? Or was he behind all the horrible things that had been happening to her?

She wouldn't put it past him to try to kill Cooper. It was bad enough that he'd spoken to him the way he had all those years ago, telling him that he wasn't good enough for her.

She was the one who wasn't good enough for him. He was a fearless hero and she had been a coward, hiding behind his protection.

A door creaked and she jumped—every bit that coward yet. Should she hide until she was sure it was who she'd called to meet her? Should she grab that urn to use as a weapon? She shuddered at the thought of touching it.

"Tanya?" a male voice called out. "Ms. Chesterfield?"

She wasn't Ms. Chesterfield anymore. She was Mrs. Payne. But she hadn't had time to legally change her name, which was good since she wasn't going to keep it anyway. "I'm in here, Mr. Gregory."

Footsteps pounded on the marble as he headed down the hall toward her. "It's quite early, Ms. Chesterfield," he protested. He looked tired with dark circles rimming his eyes, and his gray hair was mussed as if he hadn't bothered to comb it. "We could have scheduled a meeting later in the day."

"Thank you for meeting me now," she said. And for meeting her here, so she knew exactly what she was giving up: nothing. "It really couldn't wait."

"If you want to collect your inheritance today, that's not possible," he said. "It's too big an amount to be easily liquidated. And of course it needs to be divided, with half being held in trust for your sister in the event that she marries before she turns thirty."

"She can have it all," Tanya said. Then and only then did Tanya suspect that the attempts on her life and Cooper's life would stop.

Mr. Gregory shook his head. "She is unmarried. Your grandfather's will stipulates that she, too, must be married before she inherits."

"Then put it all in trust for her." She suspected Rochelle would soon be planning her wedding—if the money was really what she wanted.

Or was it Stephen?

The lawyer tensed. "What are you saying exactly?"

"I'm saying that I don't want my grandfather's money," she said, and guilt and regret overwhelmed her. "I never should have married to get it in the first place."

"I thought that was why you were marrying that Stephen fellow," Mr. Gregory, "just to inherit the money. But the Payne kid…"

"That's why I'm giving it back," she said. Although technically she'd never really had it and may not have had access to it for a while. Maybe it was a good thing that she had never received that ransom demand. Because how would she have paid it?

"You really want to give it back?" he asked. And his shoulders and back relaxed, the tension apparently leaving his body.

Why was he so relieved?

"Is that possible?" she asked. "Technically I had satisfied the stipulations of Grandfather's will before my thirtieth birthday." Today was her birthday.

He waved his hand, dismissing what his employer had wanted. "You can sign a paper claiming that the marriage was never consummated and get it annulled."

Heat flushed her face. "But what if it was?"

"It won't be a problem," he said, and there was a tone to his voice now—an edge she had never noticed before.

To have worked with her grandfather for as many years as he had, he had to have few principles or morals. But could he be...

Was he a killer?

Maybe Cooper's suspicious nature had rubbed off on her; maybe when they'd made love...

Because it made no sense to doubt a man she had known most of her life—especially since he had nothing to gain. But she had goose bumps rising on her skin. It wasn't the cold that had gotten to her. It was this horrible sense of foreboding. Her instincts warned her to get out of the mausoleum before she wound up in an urn like her grandfather.

"Well, if it's no problem, I should be going," she said. But he stood between her and the door. And she was reluctant to walk any closer to him.

"You'll need to sign those papers," he said.

"I'm sure you don't have them with you," she said. "You can draw them up and get them to me another day."

He patted his suitcase. "Actually, I do have them with me."

That seemed too convenient.

She shivered as her unease turned into fright. She was alone with a killer. And her first thought wasn't for her own safety but for Cooper's.

He would never forgive himself if she died when he was supposed to be protecting her. He would blame himself for letting her slip out while he slept. She hoped that he had at least heard her whispered words of love. Because she doubted she would have the chance to tell him again how she felt.

She wasn't certain if Mr. Gregory carried contracts in his briefcase or a gun.

But she wasn't going to wait to find out. She couldn't run for the door, so she turned and ran deeper into the shadows of the mausoleum. But even if she found a place to hide, she couldn't stay there forever.

Eventually Mr. Gregory would find her.

Chapter Seventeen

Cooper's head pounded with pain while his heart pounded with fear. Even though this warehouse looked more deserted and dangerous than the one the night before had, he wasn't concerned for his safety. He was worried about Tanya's.

Sure, Candace was a good bodyguard. But the body she was guarding was too important for Cooper to trust to anyone else. He never should have fallen asleep. But because he had, maybe she was safer with Candace.

"This place has been completely abandoned," Logan said, his voice emanating from the cell clutched in Cooper's hand.

He silently agreed, but Parker chimed in through the two-way, "This is it—the place where my informant saw the black car with the flats."

"Let's go in, then," he said. He didn't have the loading docks this time. Logan had taken that side of the building. He did have a service door—one that was so rusted, he doubted the hinges would hold it in the frame despite the lock. So he kicked it on that side and knocked it loose.

His gun drawn in front of him, he stepped inside the dark building. But after a few minutes his eyes adjusted to the faint light coming through holes rotted through the metal roof.

"Do you see anything?" Logan asked. Something rattled in the phone; he was obviously struggling hard with his doors.

A faint pounding echoed the rattling. Parker must have been struggling, too.

Cooper moved through the maze of stuff left in the building. "Just crates."

And twisted hunks of metal and other debris.

But the light illuminated a strange patch of concrete where the dust had been cleared away. He stepped closer to the crate and the pounding grew louder.

It emanated from the box. The nails on the end of it were fresh, not rusted like the others. What the hell was in the box?

He'd seen too many IEDs in Afghanistan to haphazardly bust open the crate. It could have been a trick— a setup like the forklift. If he opened that newly nailed shut side, it might explode—like so many other explosions he'd seen.

He hesitated and leaned his head against the splintered wood. The pounding in the box echoed the pounding in his head. But then he heard something else—a weak voice calling out, "Help…"

"What did you find?" Parker asked as he joined him beside the box.

Cooper holstered his gun and concentrated on the crate. "Find a crowbar—a screwdriver, something. We've gotta get this open." He clawed at the wood with his hands, driving slivers of that wood into his fingers.

"I got a crowbar," Logan said. He must have had to use one to open the loading dock doors. "What do you need it for?"

Cooper grabbed the bar and wedged it between the

wood, pulling up those newly hammered nails until the side cracked open. His brothers grabbed it and tore it off.

A man was curled up in that crate—his face crusted with blood like his matted hair. It had once been blond but now it was dark with blood. So much blood...

He peered up at Cooper through swollen eyes. "Coop?"

"Call an ambulance," he yelled at his brothers.

Parker already had his cell pressed to his ear. "It could be a while before they make it to this side of town. Should we drive him in?"

Cooper wasn't sure he should move him. But the man moved himself and crawled out of the box onto the concrete floor.

He dropped to his knees beside his old friend. "Stephen, take it easy. Don't move."

But Stephen clutched at Cooper's hand. And guilt clutched at Cooper's heart. How had he thought his friend at all responsible for the attempts on his life and Tanya's? How had he married the man's fiancé while Stephen had been locked up in this crate?

Because believing the worst of Stephen had made it easier for Cooper to act on his feelings for Tanya.

"Do you have some water in the car?" he asked Logan.

His oldest brother nodded. "I'll get it and the first-aid kit."

"And I'll wave down the ambulance," Parker said, before following his twin out of the warehouse—leaving Cooper alone with his old best friend.

"You're going to be okay," he assured him. The wound on Stephen's head still oozed blood. He must have been hit hard—hard enough to spray his blood across the wall of the groom's quarters. "Did you see who hit you?"

It wasn't Tanya, as his brothers had suspected. He was done doubting his friends.

"No…" Stephen moaned as if the sound of his own voice reverberated inside his injured head. How had he handled the sound of his own pounding echoing inside the crate?

"You don't know who did this to you?"

"I know…"

Hope quickened Cooper's pulse. "You know? But you said you didn't see him…" Nobody could press charges on suspicions and doubts; the police and prosecutors needed evidence, like eyewitness testimony.

Stephen tried to speak again, but his voice cracked. His throat was probably as dry as his peeling lips. Cooper's heart wrenched with emotion over how badly Stephen had been hurt. And then he'd been nailed up in a box and left to die.

Footsteps pounded on the concrete as someone hurriedly approached. Cooper glanced up, hoping it was the medics. But it was Logan, carrying a bottle of water. "They're only a few minutes out."

He hoped Stephen had those minutes left…after days of his wound being untreated and being dehydrated. Cooper took the water bottle from Logan, uncapped it and held it to Stephen's lips. He trickled only a little bit into his mouth.

Stephen coughed and sputtered.

Cooper cursed and hoped he hadn't done more damage to his battered friend. What if he aspirated?

But Stephen caught his breath and his voice was clearer when he spoke, "More…"

Cooper trickled more water into his open mouth.

He coughed again but not as violently.

"The ambulance will be here soon," Cooper assured him. "The docs will make you well again."

"Safe…" Stephen murmured.

"You're safe," he promised. "Nobody's going to get to you again." If Cooper would have agreed to be his best man, nobody would have gotten to Stephen the first time. Guilt gnawed at him more than the pain in his ribs and back.

Logan, ever the detective, asked, "Do you know who did this to you?"

Wanting Stephen to save his strength, Cooper answered for him, "He didn't see him."

"At the church," Stephen murmured. "I didn't see him at the church…"

Logan cursed in frustration.

"But I saw him," Stephen said, "when he opened the trunk. I saw him…"

"Who?" Cooper asked. "Who did this to you?"

"Arthur Gregory…"

"Tanya's grandfather's lawyer?" Cooper asked.

Logan cursed again.

"What?" Cooper asked his brother. "I thought you barely knew the guy."

"That's not it." A muscle twitched along Logan's tightly clenched jaw.

And Cooper's heart lurched in his chest as the horrible realization dawned on him. "Tanya's with him?"

"Candace just reported in that the lawyer showed up at the mausoleum."

"Did she stop him from going inside with Tanya?"

Logan shook her head. "I—I advised her not to."

Cooper cursed him.

"I didn't think the man was a threat," Logan said. "What's his motive?"

"Money," Stephen murmured. "I think he took the money…"

And his embezzlement would have gone undetected

if neither Chesterfield heir married before she turned thirty. "Tell Candace to get inside—to protect Tanya!"

His cell already in his hand, Logan nodded. But the phone rang and rang. "She's not picking up…"

"Go," Stephen told him. "You go…to her."

Parker wove through the crates, shoving some aside to make room for the stretcher the EMTs carried. "They're here!"

"Go," Stephen urged him again. "Go to Tanya…"

His heart was already pulling him away—toward the door, toward Tanya. But he told his brothers, "Make sure they take care of him."

"I'm going with you," Logan said. "Parker will ride along to the hospital with Stephen."

Cooper didn't care who did what as long as Mr. Gregory wasn't hurting Tanya. But the mausoleum was on the other side of town. His odds of getting there in time to protect her were pretty damn slim.

He'd been a fool to let her out of his sight—because he might never see her again. Alive.

DUST FILLED HER lungs, making it hard to draw air into them. Her nose tickled and throat burned, but she couldn't sneeze. She couldn't cough. She couldn't even breathe hard for fear that he might find where she was hiding.

She had crawled into a tall cabinet in the butler's pantry. With her knees pressed against her chest and the back of her head pressed against the top of the cabinet, the hard wood was unrelenting against her skull.

The cabinet's door wasn't that thick, so she could hear through it. A door creaked open—maybe the kitchen door—since it was loud enough to reach her ears. And a female voice—maybe Candace—called out her name. "Tanya?"

Something hard and metallic dropped, and it clanged

against the kitchen tiles. Then something heavier struck the ground, too, with a dull thump.

She wanted to call back. But she doubted Candace could hear her now. Had Mr. Gregory killed her?

Tears stung her eyes and burned the back of her throat. But she struggled to contain them. She couldn't give away her hiding place.

"It's useless to try to hide from me," he yelled, his voice alarmingly close.

She sucked in her breath and held it—until her lungs ached.

"I will find you."

He knew she had figured it out because she'd run. She shouldn't have run from him. But she'd only ever been able to hide her feelings from one person—Cooper. Everyone else was able to tell what she was thinking; they could see through her lies.

But what was the point of killing her? Then Cooper, as her husband, would gain her inheritance. Unless he intended to kill Cooper, too.

If only she could get to a weapon…

Maybe the metallic thing that had fallen was Candace's gun. If she could sneak past Mr. Gregory…

"Where the hell are you?" the man shouted, but his voice was fainter as he moved farther away from her. Then she heard footsteps pounding across that marble foyer and then up the marble stairs. Those footsteps moved overhead.

She drew in a breath and pushed open that cupboard door. Her leg muscles twinged as she unfolded them and crawled out of the small space. They nearly gave as she dropped onto the counter and then the floor below that.

She moved on tiptoe across the butler's pantry toward the kitchen, not wanting her own footsteps echoing throughout the empty mansion. Candace had crumpled onto the kitchen floor, a wound on her head oozing blood onto the dingy white tiles. Tanya pressed her fingers to the woman's neck, feeling for a pulse. When she felt the telltale flutter, she breathed a sigh of relief.

But then she glanced around her. If Candace had had a gun, it was gone. Mr. Gregory must have taken it.

Candace was too statuesque for Tanya to move her; she couldn't carry the woman outside and she couldn't leave her here—at Mr. Gregory's mercy.

"Candace?" she whispered. "Wake up..."

The woman shifted, but she didn't regain consciousness. She had moved enough that her pant leg slid up. Metal glinted off a gun strapped to her ankle.

Her fingers trembling, Tanya reached for it but fumbled with the holster clasp.

Footsteps echoed off the marble again. He was coming.

She grabbed at the gun and whirled around with it clutched in her hands.

"At least this time you have the safety on," Cooper remarked. "So you won't blow my head off."

"She won't, but I will," Mr. Gregory said.

Cooper turned toward the man who'd sneaked up behind him. His back was to Tanya now, but for that split second before he'd turned, she'd seen his face. He hadn't seemed very surprised that Mr. Gregory had just threatened to kill him.

He'd figured out what she had.

"Nobody needs to get shot here," he said. He glanced down at the floor. "You didn't shoot Candace?"

"He must have hit her over the head," Tanya said. If only she had warned Candace...

"Like he did Stephen."

"You found Stephen?" she asked. "Is he...?"

"He's still alive," Cooper replied, but he spoke to Mr. Gregory now. "And soon he'll be well enough to testify against you."

The lawyer shrugged. "I will be long gone before I'll be arrested."

"Then just leave," Cooper suggested. "Just walk away right now."

"You'd like that," Mr. Gregory said. "You've been messing up my plans since you got back in the country."

"Your plan was to kill Tanya?"

"That only became necessary when you decided to become her white knight," Mr. Gregory said.

Cooper was acting as her white knight now because he had positioned his body between her and the deranged lawyer and his gun. The barrel was pointed at Cooper's chest now.

"All I wanted to do was stop her from marrying," Mr. Gregory explained, "Stephen Wochholz or anyone else."

Tanya shuddered.

"You didn't want her to inherit the money," Cooper said.

"What money?" Mr. Gregory asked with a chuckle. "The money's gone."

Tanya gasped in surprise. He had embezzled all of it.

"Then it's over," Cooper said. "Just leave. Take whatever you've got left and leave the country."

"I will leave," Mr. Gregory assured them, "as soon as I get rid of you."

Fear overwhelming her, she gasped again. "No!"

"Why are you acting like you care now?" Mr. Gregory taunted her. "You were so desperate a little while ago to get your annulment that you were willing to give up your inheritance to end your marriage."

Cooper tensed. Was he offended? Hurt?

"You hurt Stephen and you kept trying to hurt Cooper," she said, trying to explain why she'd done what she had. To keep him safe…

"Kept trying?" the lawyer scoffed. "I tried to push a car on him."

"But all the gunshots," she said, "at Stephen's condo and at his brother, who you must have mistaken for Cooper…"

"I fired into your apartment but that was to hit you—after he stopped me from running you over." The lawyer snarled. "He kept stopping me…when he saved you from the asthma attack and the peanut allergy. Your sister helped with that. Maybe I should take care of her, too, before I leave the country.

"Nobody else needs to get hurt," Cooper said. "Stephen's going to make it. You haven't killed anyone. So there'll be no murder charges."

"Just attempted murder," the lawyer said. "And embezzlement. I might as well commit murder, too. And for all the times you've messed up my plan, I really, really want to kill you, Cooper Payne."

"No!" Tanya shouted.

But the gun was already raised. Mr. Gregory squeezed the trigger. And a shot rang out.

Chapter Eighteen

Tanya's scream rang in Cooper's ears. The terror in it chilled his blood. But it wasn't his blood that was spilled across the white tile floor. Mr. Gregory lay lifelessly in front of him—a bullet in his head.

"Everybody okay?" Logan asked from behind him. Cooper had distracted the man so his brother could get in place to take the shot—if he needed to. Since the lawyer had been squeezing the trigger, Cooper was fortunate that Logan was a damn good shot. Or he might have an actual hole in his heart instead of just a figurative one.

"Yeah, thanks," Cooper said.

"You could sound a little more grateful," Logan teased as he dropped to his knees and took Candace's pulse. Their family usually handled every emotion with humor; otherwise they would have never survived the loss of their father. Maybe Logan had gotten so good at coping that he didn't betray any other emotions. Or he kept everything inside. "Her pulse is strong."

"I'm strong," Candace murmured as she regained consciousness. "I can beat you arm wrestling."

He chuckled. "Good thing he hit you in the head—since it's so hard."

Cooper hoped her heart was hard, too. Because it was obvious that Logan didn't return the feelings she had for her boss. His big brother couldn't have gotten that good at hiding his emotions. Because if Cooper had found Tanya lying on the floor like that, he wouldn't have been able to tease. His hands would have been shaking too badly to take the shot that Logan had. His heart clutched with sympathy for Candace because he knew how badly it hurt when someone didn't love you the way you loved them.

Tanya wanted a divorce so desperately that she'd been willing to give up her inheritance.

Her hands clutched his shoulder. "Cooper, are you all right?" she asked.

He shrugged off her touch. "Fine." And because he cared so much, he turned and reached out to her. But he didn't pull her into his arms as he longed to do. Instead, he just touched her hair, brushing cobwebs and dust from the silken strands. "Are you okay?"

"Yeah…" She expelled a shaky sigh. "When I realized everything…I ran and hid."

"What were you thinking to meet him here?" he asked. "Alone?" But he knew. She was thinking she wanted to get rid of her husband. And she hadn't cared how much it would cost her. Even her life?

"I didn't know he was the one…behind everything…"

"But you shouldn't have gone off alone," he reminded her. His guts clenched with dread. He hated to think of what could have happened to her—of how she could have been the one lying on the floor—either with a wound on her head or a bullet in it. "It's hard to protect someone who won't let you."

"It's over now," she said. "I don't need your protection anymore."

"No," he agreed. She obviously didn't need him anymore.

"Is it over?" Logan asked the question now. "Gregory

said he only fired those shots at your apartment. He admitted to everything else, so why would he lie about those other times? Parker got shot at outside Stephen's place."

"And you got shot at, too," Cooper remarked as his head began to pound again.

"But I was posing as you," Logan said.

Despite the pounding, Cooper shook his head. "You and Parker can pass as each other. I'm not so sure anyone would have really been fooled into thinking you were me." Then maybe those shots outside Stephen's had really been meant for Parker and hadn't been just because he'd gone out the door first.

"Do you think there's someone else?" Tanya asked with a shudder. "That Mr. Gregory was working with someone else?"

Candace had managed to sit up and lean against the wall behind her. "It's more likely that the someone else has nothing to do with you."

Tanya turned to Cooper, her eyes wide with concern. "Someone else is trying to kill you?"

"Not me," he assured her. "I just got back into the country." And his enemies wouldn't have been able to follow him here. "This is about something else..." Logan. "It doesn't concern you."

A twinge of disappointment squeezed her heart. He had just reminded her that she wasn't really part of his family. They'd only been married a couple of days before she'd decided to end it.

Sirens wailed outside the mausoleum. "As soon as the police are done taking our report, I'll bring you to the hospital to see Stephen."

"Uh, Stephen, of course." She lifted trembling fingers to her face and brushed away another cobweb. "Is he really going to be all right?"

"He's strong to have survived the head wound and all those days of being nailed inside a crate," he said.

She moved her hand to her mouth, as if to hold in another scream.

"And I'm sure he'll be even better once we get our divorce and you can marry him."

She loved Stephen, but she didn't want to marry him. She wanted to stay married to her husband because she was in love with him. Cooper obviously didn't return those feelings. He hadn't even come with her to the hospital. He'd sent her in the ambulance with Candace.

After Candace had been taken for a CT scan, Tanya had found Stephen's hospital room. The minute she stepped inside, she reached out and clutched his hand.

"Don't!" Rochelle yelled at her from where she sat on the other side of Stephen's bed.

He cried out, and Tanya pulled back. Seeing how raw his fingers were, he must have been digging at something. The crate Cooper said he'd found him nailed inside...

She shuddered over the horrors her dear friend had been forced to endure—because of her. "I'm sorry. I'm *so* sorry..."

"You should be sorry," Rochelle snapped at her. "You did all this for nothing—for money that was already gone."

Nikki must have called and filled in her friend about Mr. Gregory. It had been him acting alone in the attempts on her life and Stephen's. Cooper had lifted the lawyer's sleeves to reveal her scratches on his arms. And they'd found evidence that the tear-gas container had been inside his briefcase.

Tears of regret stung Tanya's eyes.

"It's not your fault," Stephen said. "It was my plan that we get married."

Rochelle gasped. "It was?"

"Your sister didn't want the money, but I pointed out everything she could do with it—all the people she could help."

Rochelle's lips curved into the first genuine smile Tanya had seen on her face since she was a child. "Of course it was your plan. You are such a sweet man."

Stephen reached his injured hand out to Tanya's little sister, and he patted her cheek. "You're pretty sweet yourself."

Rochelle? What kind of painkillers had they given him?

Rochelle giggled like the child she'd once been before she'd become a bitter, angry adult. "I'm anything but sweet—Tanya will tell you that. I've been a complete witch to her."

"You didn't know," Stephen said. "I should have told you…"

"Did you know?" Rochelle asked.

Tanya furrowed her brow with confusion. Was her sister drunk? "It was *his* plan."

"Not the plan," Rochelle said with another delighted giggle. "His feelings…"

"Do you mind if I tell her alone?" Stephen asked.

Rochelle nodded and walked out of the room as if she were floating a few feet above the ground.

"Tell me what?" Tanya asked.

"I love your sister."

"You what?" She had never noticed anything romantic between the two.

"I love Rochelle," he said.

She was stunned. "When you disappeared, I realized she had feelings for you, but…"

"I didn't realize it either until I was locked up in that

crate," he said. "Hers was the face I most wanted to see again. Hers the voice I most wanted to hear."

Tanya uttered a wistful sigh, longing for someone to love her like that. And for that someone to be Cooper.

"I'm sorry," he said.

"You have no reason to be sorry," she assured him. "You and I were never anything more than friends."

"You, me and Cooper—the three amigos," he said with a chuckle. "But you and him were never just friends. He married you."

She nodded. "Just so I would be able to inherit and pay a ransom in case one was made for your return."

"I heard he had some doubts about my part in all of this," Stephen said. Obviously Rochelle had told him everything that had happened in his absence. "So maybe he had another reason to marry you."

"For my protection," she said. "Mr. Gregory was trying to kill me."

"You wished it was real, though," he said. "You love Cooper. You always have."

But it was even more hopeless than it had been when they were teenagers. "It doesn't matter," she said, her voice cracking with emotion, "because he doesn't love me. He'll never love…" She dropped into the chair beside his bed and her shoulders shook as she wept.

With his injured hand, Stephen patted her hair.

She should have been the one comforting him after everything he'd endured. But, as usual, he was the one offering her comfort.

"I really love you," she told him.

A noise drew her attention to the door—where Cooper stood. Before she could call out to him, he turned and left, the door swinging shut behind him. He obviously thought she was in love with Stephen. But what did that matter to Cooper since he didn't love her?

"So you wouldn't stand up as my best man, but you want a favor from me!" Stephen exclaimed as he slammed the door to Cooper's office and strode up to his desk.

Coop was officially part of the Payne Protection team and as a family member as well as an employee he'd been given an office—a dark-paneled room that was smaller than Logan's and Parker's but bigger than the cubby they'd given Nikki.

"I thought it was a favor you'd want, too." Given what Cooper had seen and heard a couple of days ago in Stephen's hospital room.

The man had healed quickly—probably because he had someone waiting for him. But he still had a bandage on his head to protect the stitches that had finally stopped the bleeding. And he had dark circles rimming his eyes that were now wide in shock. "You think I want to draw up your divorce papers?"

"I think you want me to divorce Tanya," Cooper admitted with a trace of bitterness. Maybe he was more petty than he'd thought since he couldn't bring himself to be happy for his friends.

"Why?" Stephen asked.

"So you can marry her." Nikki had gone running out minutes ago to meet Tanya and Rochelle at the church to make wedding arrangements with his mother. Apparently Tanya was so anxious to marry Stephen that she'd forgotten that she was still married to Cooper.

He hadn't forgotten. He hadn't forgotten anything about her. The smell of her hair. The taste of her lips. The way she felt when he buried himself deep inside her— the heat and closeness of her body holding him tightly.

He'd felt as if they had become one, just as the minister had said when he'd married them. But Cooper hadn't seen his wife since he'd heard her declaring her love for another man.

Stephen chuckled. "Everybody said that you would change so much once you became a Marine. And after you got deployed…"

He had changed, but for the most part he thought he did a pretty good job of holding back the memories and the nightmares. Even though Stephen was about to marry the woman Cooper loved, he was his friend. So Coop admitted, "I have changed."

Stephen shook his head. "No, you haven't. You're the same fool you've always been…"

"You're the fool," Cooper said, "to come to my office and insult me."

"You called me here with that stupid voice mail you left, asking me to draw up divorce papers for you and Tanya."

He shrugged. "Annulment papers, then. I'll sign whatever Tanya wants."

"Do you know what Tanya wants?"

"You."

Stephen chuckled again. "She told you that?"

He thought back, trying to remember their conversations. "She told the lawyer she wanted to divorce me."

"Did she tell you why?"

"Because she doesn't want to be married to me," Cooper said.

"Did she tell you that?"

His ribs and back hurt less, but now the pain was throbbing in his head. "Why do you keep asking me all these questions?"

"Because I want to make sure you really know what's in Tanya's heart and you're not just assuming."

I love you...

But he had only dreamed that she'd whispered those words in his ear. He had been completely awake when he'd heard her declare her feelings for Stephen.

"I'm not just assuming," he insisted. "I know…"

"Do you know what's in *your* heart?" Stephen asked.

Cooper snorted. He was not going to have this conversation with the man who was about marry the woman he loved.

"I didn't know what was in mine," Stephen admitted. "I didn't know until I had all those days in the box to think about it."

"Are you suggesting I nail myself inside a box?"

Stephen grimaced.

"Too soon?" he teased.

"Just a little bit." But Stephen grinned. "I've missed you, my friend."

And because they were friends, Cooper had to do this. "Draw up the papers for me."

Stephen reluctantly nodded. "If that's what you really want, I will."

Cooper sucked in a breath over the pain of the jab in his heart. "Okay…"

"But I won't do it until you talk to Tanya."

"That's not necessary."

"It is if you want me to do this favor for you," Stephen said. "You have to do this favor for me."

"Talking to Tanya is doing a favor for *you?*"

Stephen grinned. "Yes, and it's a favor that can't wait. You need to talk to her now."

"But she's at the church." Planning his wedding.

"Exactly. You've already wasted enough time," Stephen

admonished him. "Talk to her and then tell me if you want these papers drawn up…"

He didn't want them at all. He didn't want to divorce Tanya. But he couldn't stay married to a woman who loved another man. It was time to end his marriage.

Chapter Nineteen

Tanya found it hard to focus on the wedding plans the others were discussing in Mrs. Payne's sunbathed sunshine-yellow office. She could only hear Cooper's voice ringing in her head from the message he'd left on Stephen's phone. She'd been with her friend when he'd played his voice mail. "I need you to draw up my divorce papers..."

He'd promised that he would end their marriage. And Cooper Payne was a man of his word. She felt like a hypocrite—planning a wedding while her own marriage was ending.

Rochelle nudged her shoulder. "I need your opinion," she said. "You're my maid of honor."

"Matron," Mrs. Payne corrected her. "Your sister is married, so she's a matron."

She wasn't going to be married much longer if Cooper had his way.

Rochelle giggled. She did that so often now, since she was giddy with happiness. "If only she were a little more matronly, I would look better."

"You're going to look beautiful," Tanya assured her. "You are beautiful. Radiant even."

Rochelle blushed. "You're a good matron of honor."

Tanya had been so touched that her sister had asked

her, that she was making an effort to end their resentment and misunderstandings and finally form a real sisterly bond. To ensure Rochelle's happiness, she had to put aside her own pain and loss.

"I'm so happy for you both," she said.

Rochelle leaned over and squeezed Tanya's hand. "You could be this happy, too."

"I just told you, I'm happy."

"For me and Stephen. I want you to be happy for yourself," Rochelle said. "Tell Cooper how you feel about him."

She had. But she'd just cowardly whispered the words in his ear. "It doesn't matter..."

"Why not?"

"Because he doesn't feel the same."

"How do you feel about my son?" Mrs. Payne asked with a big smile that suggested that she knew exactly how Tanya felt about Cooper and that she had probably always known.

"How do you?" a deep voice asked. And his tone suggested that he did not know.

He must not have heard those words she'd whispered in his ear that night. "I told you," she said.

"When I was sleeping..."

So he had heard her.

"But I still told you," she insisted. "What about you?" She gathered the courage to finally ask what she'd been dying for years to know. "How do you feel about me?"

And she held her breath, waiting for his answer.

And waiting...

HEAT CLIMBED INTO Cooper's neck as he realized all these women were staring at him. His mother. His sister. Her sister. And Tanya...

She had really said those words; he hadn't just imagined them. She loved him.

"I heard you tell Stephen the same thing," he said.

"I do love Stephen. But like a friend," she clarified. "Not like Rochelle loves him. Not like he loves Rochelle."

And then he got it. "It's their wedding you're here planning."

Rochelle grinned. "You thought she was planning a wedding to Stephen. She's not a bigamist."

"He called Stephen to draw up divorce papers," she shared with her sister.

"He wouldn't do it until I came here and talked to you," he admitted.

"So you're only here because of Stephen."

He was losing her. He felt it, felt her slipping away. "When you said those words to me, did you mean them the same way you said them to Stephen?"

She made him wait. Her body tense, lips pursed as she considered whether or not to answer him. He didn't blame her if she didn't. He'd just told her that he only came here to get divorce papers drawn up. It would take a lot of courage for her to put herself out there first. But Tanya was much stronger than she looked.

"I have never felt about you like I do Stephen," she said. "You and I have never been just friends. At least not on my end."

"Not on my end either," he admitted.

She waited again.

And he hesitated. He had never been a coward before. He hadn't hesitated to join the Marines. He hadn't hesitated to engage in combat. But he hesitated now because Tanya could hurt him more than any bullet or bomb. She'd said the words, but that didn't mean they had a future together. "Your grandfather was right all those years ago. I had nothing to offer you. I have nothing to offer you now either."

"Yes, you do," she said. "You're just not willing to offer it."

"I have no money."

"I don't either," she reminded him. "I've been fine without money."

"Then why were you going to marry Stephen to collect it?"

"She had plans for the money," Rochelle answered for her. "She was going to help people."

Of course she was. No wonder he loved her so much.

"She doesn't need the money to help people," he said.

Rochelle nodded in agreement. "But there actually is some left. Stephen found Mr. Gregory's offshore accounts. And there's already been an offer on Grandfather's house."

Tanya turned toward her sister, her brow furrowing with confusion. "Who would want that thing?"

"A funeral home."

She laughed in delight.

She would inherit some money now since she'd married before her birthday. Would it be enough to put her out of his league again?

"I don't need money," she said as if she could read his mind.

He actually had more than she or his family probably realized. Because he'd needed very little to live on, he'd invested what he'd been paid, and given the bonuses for every time he'd re-upped, it had mounted.

"What about love?" he asked her. "Do you need love?"

Her breath audibly caught and her green eyes widened with surprise and hope. "Do you…?"

"Love you?" He nodded. "Only with all my heart and soul."

"Well, if that's all…" She jumped up from her chair and threw her arms around his neck. She pressed a kiss to his cheek and his chin and his nose. "I love you! I love you!"

"Yeah, yeah," Nikki said, feigning disinterest despite her sparkling eyes. "Tell us something we haven't all known for years and years…"

Cooper laughed. "I want to do it again."

"What?"

"I want to marry you again," he said.

"Another wedding?" his little sister asked. "It's like you know someone who owns a wedding chapel or something…"

"Yeah, it's like…"

His mother chuckled as she always had at the teasing bickering of her children. That was why they'd started doing it so much—to make her laugh.

Tanya pulled out of his arms. "We can't!"

And panic clutched his heart. Had she changed her mind? Did she not feel strongly enough about him to marry him again?

"We can't infringe on Rochelle's day," she said. "This is her time."

"Finally," Rochelle murmured. "We've both taken our time getting here. How about we walk down that aisle together?" she asked Tanya. "We'll give each other away to the men we love."

Two brides and two grooms stood at the altar. There were two best men—so identical in their black tuxes that it was impossible for Tanya to tell one from the other. Until Parker winked at her.

She and Rochelle shared a maid of honor. Nikki juggled both their bouquets. Tanya's was simple and small—just a bunch of yellow roses—while Rochelle's was a trailing mass of colors and textures.

Rochelle's dress was also nontraditional—short and ruffled and the same blush as the color on her smiling cheeks. Since Rochelle had had time to find that dress, Tanya might have been able to find a new one, too.

But there was only one dress she'd wanted to wear on her wedding day. And thankfully the paramedics hadn't damaged it. She wore Mrs. Payne's—Mom's, as Penny now insisted she call her—beautiful beaded lace gown.

Tanya had worried during the few shorts days it had taken Mrs. Payne—*Mom*—to pull together the weddings that she was infringing on Rochelle's day. But her little sister was happier than Tanya had ever seen her. And so was Stephen as he slid his ring on her finger.

Then it was Cooper's turn. He took her hand in his. Her skin tingled from his touch—and from the intensity of his blue eyes as he gazed down at her.

"With this ring, I thee wed," he repeated as he slid a gold and sparkling diamond band onto her finger.

She marveled at the beauty of it. She had known Cooper since they were both kids, but the man could still surprise her. Like when he added his own vows: "I will love and protect you for the rest of my life, Tanya Payne."

Tanya Payne.

"I love the sound of that," she murmured. "I love you. Always have and always will. You are my best friend. My soul mate. My everything…"

Cooper blinked his thick lashes as if he, too, was battling tears. Of emotion. Of love.

"I now pronounce both couples men and wives," Reverend James said with a chuckle.

Stephen kissed his bride. And Cooper lowered his head to Tanya's, his lips pressing tenderly against hers in such a sweet and gentle kiss that tears sprung to her eyes.

"There'll be more kissing later," he promised her in a whisper for her ears only.

She couldn't wait for later. The reception passed in a blur of eating and dancing and laughing. This was the wedding she had always wanted. And it was all the sweeter that she was able to share it with her sister, her friends and her new family.

Parker twirled her around the dance floor. "This wedding's been kind of boring," he complained with a teasing grin. "Nobody's gotten kidnapped, shot at or poisoned."

Tanya blew out a breath of relief that none of those things had happened. Because usually those things happened to her or Cooper. "I don't know what you're talking about," she teased back as the Payne family—*her* family—loved to tease. "It's been the most exciting day of my life."

Cooper tugged her out of his brother's arms and swung her up in his own. "It's about to get more exciting," he said, "we're heading off for our honeymoon now."

Stephen and Rochelle had already left—eager to start the life together that had nearly been denied them. She forced back the guilt and regret. The past was over. Everyone was safe and happy.

"I hope you packed some of that sexy lingerie," Cooper said.

"Oh, I have something special for you," she promised.

"You're the something special," he said.

She clasped her arms around her husband's neck as he carried her up the steps from the lower-level reception hall. He passed through the vestibule and headed down the outside church staircase to the street.

Logan and Nikki stood on the steps, leaning against the railing. Laughing, they flung handfuls of birdseed at them as Cooper and Tanya passed. Parker followed behind, tossing it down on them like rain. An SUV waited at the curb. Across its back window someone had scrawled *Just Married* in chalk. And strings of pop cans had been tied to the back bumper.

"Damn you all!" Cooper playfully yelled at his family.

Tanya laughed, happier than she had ever been.

Until the shots rang out…

Cooper ducked low over Tanya, protecting her with his body and the SUV that he shielded them both behind. But his family—their family—stood on the front steps yet, exposed.

Tires squealed as the car from which the shots must have been fired sped around the corner. She wriggled out of Cooper's arms and turned back.

Logan covered Nikki on the stairs. But Parker was gone.

"Parker!" Cooper yelled his name as he hurried over to the stairs. A hand rose from the thick shrubs on the sides of the stairwell. He clasped it and pulled his brother from the foliage. "You okay?"

"Yeah, yeah," he said, brushing off his tux and their concern. "Logan knocked me over after pushing down Nikki." He turned toward his twin, as if waiting for the smart-alecky comments they continually threw at each other.

But Logan said nothing but sorry. He said it to his brother and sister and then he turned to Tanya and Cooper. "I'm sorry…"

Tanya shook her head. "I thought it was over. Mr. Gregory is dead." But maybe he hadn't been working alone.

"This isn't about you," Logan assured them all. "This is about me. And revenge…"

"You know who it is," Cooper said.

He nodded. "And I'll take care of it. You two leave for your honeymoon." He hugged them both then pushed them toward the SUV. "Leave before the police get here. You've given enough reports during the past week to last a lifetime."

Cooper obeyed his brother and helped Tanya into the passenger's seat before sliding behind the wheel himself. She clutched his arm. "Are you sure?" she asked. "If you want to stay and help him, our honeymoon can wait."

"Our honeymoon waited too long," he said, "because of my stubbornness and pride." He glanced back at his family. "They trusted me to take care of myself while I was in the Marines. I trust Logan to protect himself and the others."

His brother waved them off as Cooper pulled away from the curb. Tanya stared back at them and she couldn't help worrying that it might be the last time she saw them.

Cooper took her hand in his and entwined their fingers. "They'll be okay," he promised her. "They're Paynes."

She smiled.

"And so are you," he said. "You are my wife."

"It's real," she said with a sweet sigh of relief.

"We're still going to consummate it," he teased. "Over and over again…"

She laughed. He was right. His family could take care of themselves—they'd been doing it for years. And now she and Cooper would spend the rest of their lives taking care of each other. "I love you."

"I'm not sure I heard you," he teased, probably in reference to that first time she had uttered those words to him in a whisper.

So she shouted, "I love you!"

"Married a few hours and she's already yelling at me," Cooper remarked to himself.

Tanya laughed again as she envisioned their future together, as she had so many times when she'd been a teenager. But now it wasn't just a fantasy; it was real. They probably would yell at each other from time to time. But they would have laughter, too. And given her job and his, they would probably have danger, as well. But as he'd promised, he would keep her safe. And she would make certain that he always knew how much she loved him— even if she had to shout it.

* * * * *

COMING NEXT MONTH FROM

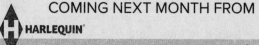

HARLEQUIN

INTRIGUE

Available June 17, 2014

#1503 WEDDING AT CARDWELL RANCH
Cardwell Cousins • by B.J. Daniels
Someone is hell-bent on making Allie Taylor think she's losing her mind. Allie's past has stalked her to Cardwell Ranch, and not even Jackson Cardwell may be able to save her from a killer with a chilling agenda.

#1504 HARD RIDE TO DRY GULCH
Big "D" Dads: The Daltons • by Joanna Wayne
Faith Ashburn turns to sexy detective Travis Dalton to find and save her missing son. In the process, will Travis lose his heart and find a family?

#1505 UNDERCOVER WARRIOR
Copper Canyon • by Aimée Thurlo
Was Agent Kyle Goodluck's last undercover assignment too close to home for comfort? Now Kyle's only hope to prevent an attack that would rock the entire nation is the mysterious woman he's just rescued from terrorists, Erin Barrett.

#1506 EXPLOSIVE ENGAGEMENT
Shotgun Weddings • by Lisa Childs
Stacy Kozminski and Logan Payne must fake an engagement to survive. But with someone trying to kill them with bullets and bombs, they may never make it to the altar.

#1507 STRANDED
The Rescuers • by Alice Sharpe
When detective Alex Foster returns from the dead, he wants two things: his estranged, pregnant wife, Jessica, to love him, and to capture the man who wants them both dead....

#1508 SANCTUARY IN CHEF VOLEUR
The Delancey Dynasty • by Mallory Kane
Hannah Martin flees to New Orleans looking for help from PI Mack Griffin. It doesn't take him long to appreciate Hannah's courage and resourcefulness, or to realize that he may end up needing protection, too—from his feelings for her. _____

HICNM0614

REQUEST YOUR FREE BOOKS!
2 FREE NOVELS PLUS 2 FREE GIFTS!

⊕ HARLEQUIN®

INTRIGUE®

BREATHTAKING ROMANTIC SUSPENSE

YES! Please send me 2 FREE Harlequin Intrigue® novels and my 2 FREE gifts (gifts are worth about $10). After receiving them, if I don't wish to receive any more books, I can return the shipping statement marked "cancel." If I don't cancel, I will receive 6 brand-new novels every month and be billed just $4.74 per book in the U.S. or $5.24 per book in Canada. That's a savings of at least 14% off the cover price! It's quite a bargain! Shipping and handling is just 50¢ per book in the U.S. and 75¢ per book in Canada.* I understand that accepting the 2 free books and gifts places me under no obligation to buy anything. I can always return a shipment and cancel at any time. Even if I never buy another book, the two free books and gifts are mine to keep forever.

182/382 HDN F42N

Name	(PLEASE PRINT)	
Address		Apt. #
City	State/Prov.	Zip/Postal Code

Signature (if under 18, a parent or guardian must sign)

Mail to the **Harlequin® Reader Service:**
IN U.S.A.: P.O. Box 1867, Buffalo, NY 14240-1867
IN CANADA: P.O. Box 609, Fort Erie, Ontario L2A 5X3
Are you a subscriber to Harlequin Intrigue books
and want to receive the larger-print edition?
Call 1-800-873-8635 or visit www.ReaderService.com.

* Terms and prices subject to change without notice. Prices do not include applicable taxes. Sales tax applicable in N.Y. Canadian residents will be charged applicable taxes. Offer not valid in Quebec. This offer is limited to one order per household. Not valid for current subscribers to Harlequin Intrigue books. All orders subject to credit approval. Credit or debit balances in a customer's account(s) may be offset by any other outstanding balance owed by or to the customer. Please allow 4 to 6 weeks for delivery. Offer available while quantities last.

Your Privacy—The Harlequin® Reader Service is committed to protecting your privacy. Our Privacy Policy is available online at www.ReaderService.com or upon request from the Harlequin Reader Service.

We make a portion of our mailing list available to reputable third parties that offer products we believe may interest you. If you prefer that we not exchange your name with third parties, or if you wish to clarify or modify your communication preferences, please visit us at www.ReaderService.com/consumerchoice or write to us at Harlequin Reader Service Preference Service, P.O. Box 9062, Buffalo, NY 14269. Include your complete name and address.

HI13R

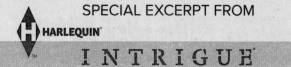
"I'm afraid to ask what you just said to your horse," Jackson joked as he moved closer. Her horse had wandered over to some tall grass away from the others.

"Just thanking him for not bucking me off," she admitted shyly.

"Probably a good idea, but your horse is a she. A mare."

"Oh, hopefully she wasn't insulted." Allie actually smiled. The afternoon sun lit her face along with the smile.

He felt his heart do a loop-de-loop. He tried to rein it back in as he looked into her eyes. That tantalizing green was deep and dark, inviting, and yet he knew a man could drown in those eyes.

Suddenly, Allie's horse shied. In the next second it took off as if it had been shot from a cannon. To her credit, she hadn't let go of her reins, but she grabbed the saddle horn and let out a cry as the mare raced out of the meadow headed for the road.

Jackson spurred his horse and raced after her. He could hear the startled cries of the others behind him. He'd been riding since he was a boy, so he knew how to handle his horse. But Allie, he could see, was having trouble staying in the saddle with her horse at a full gallop.

He pushed his horse harder and managed to catch her, riding alongside until he could reach over and grab her reins. The horses lunged along for a moment. Next to him Allie started to fall. He grabbed for her, pulling her from her saddle and into his arms as he released her reins and brought his own horse up short.

Allie slid down his horse to the ground. He dismounted and dropped beside her. "Are you all right?"

"I think so. What happened?"

He didn't know. One minute her horse was munching on grass, the next it had taken off like a shot.

Allie had no idea why the horse had reacted like that. She hated that she was the one who'd upset everyone.

"Are you sure you didn't spur your horse?" Natalie asked, still upset.

"She isn't wearing spurs," Ford pointed out.

"Maybe a bee stung your horse," Natalie suggested.

Dana felt bad. "I wanted your first horseback-riding experience to be a pleasant one," she lamented.

"It was. It is," Allie reassured her, although in truth, she wasn't looking forward to getting back on the horse. But she knew she had to for Natalie's sake. The kids had been scared enough as it was.

Dana had spread out the lunch on a large blanket with the kids all helping when Jackson rode up, trailing her horse. The mare looked calm now, but Allie wasn't sure she would ever trust it again.

Jackson met her gaze as he dismounted. Dana was already on her feet, heading for him. Allie left the kids to join them.

"What is it?" Dana asked, keeping her voice down.

Jackson looked to Allie as if he didn't want to say in front of her.

"Did I do something to the horse to make her do that?" she asked, fearing that she had.

His expression softened as he shook his head. "You didn't do *anything*." He looked at Dana. "Someone shot the mare."

Someone is hell-bent on making Allie Taylor think she's losing her mind. Jackson's determined to unmask the perp. Can he guard the widowed wedding planner and her little girl from a killer with a chilling agenda?

Find out what happens next in
WEDDING AT CARDWELL RANCH
by New York Times *bestselling author B.J. Daniels,*
available July 2014, only from Harlequin® Intrigue®.